High Fyelds

THE BIG RACE

SEVEN OF STARS

Also by Mae McKinnon

HIGH FYELDS — A NEW BEGINNING
Seven of Stars

MACIAL MISCHIEF — A MOTIONBOOK
Seven of Stars

THE DAMSEL AND THE DRAGON
Seven of Stars

ACADEMIA DRACONIA
Seven of Stars

DAWN OF THE WINDS
(credited as M. Aei)
Seven of Stars

WOLF'S BANE
(credited as M. Aei)
Seven of Stars

High Fyelds

THE BIG RACE

SEVEN OF STARS

Mae McKinnon

DRAGONQUILL PUBLISHING

High Fyelds: The Big Race
A DragonQuill book

Cover art and logo by Juliane Völker
nightpark-art.de

Cover design by Marlene Ockersse

Formatting by Marlene Ockersse

Edited by Ashley Lachance
scribecat.ca

First printed in France, 2018

ISBN 978-91-984558-1-6
A CIP catalogue record for this book is available from the National Library of Sweden

DragonQuill Publishing
www.dragonquillpublishing.wordpress.com

CHAPTERS

IF YOU ARE READING THIS,
THIS BOOK IS DEDICATED
TO YOU!

CHAPTER ONE

The world rumbled. Hooves pounded against the packed soil of the track; the thunder eating away at all other noises as the pack flew past the stands. Amongst them, the paws and pads that loped across the ground made barely any sound at all.

Not even the whine from the engines of the passenger-carrier passing above could completely drown out the sound of the race.

In front, two leaders fought neck-to-neck as they came into the homestretch. But neither racers, nor spectators, so much as twitched an ear as the leafflyer slowed — preparing to land — having long since gotten used to the daily schedule of the nearby shiport.[1] Only newcomers and tourists craned their necks to see what infernal noise was laying a short, but intense, siege to their hearing.

Not that it was the engines themselves that were actually making all the racket. Mostly it was just the wind striking the main cooling valves that was throwing its weight around, that, and the wings. And the leafflyer was almost all wing.

Not that anyone really cared — it was still noisy — but the race had most people's attention, even that of some of the passengers.

Those that *did* look up caught a glimpse of a smooth glittering silver surface. The ship was a new enough sight to most of them that it was still awe-inspiring, having been put into regular operations only a year or so before. Its

---

[1] Shiports were the ultimate hybrid — a cross between airports, spaceports and, if they were on the coast, there was a dash of port of the ship variety thrown in as well, sailing or otherwise.

flat body and small vestigial wings gave it a unique silhouette in a trade where bulk carriers plied much of the airways.

Indeed, a number of the visitors to the Epsilon Court had probably come in on one of them a day or so before. Its speed and efficiency made its range of operations cover lines on anything from town to town transportation about as effortlessly as it did the continent to continent ones. And on top of that it was a comfortable ride as well — never a bad thing — and an unusual combination in this day of age. A pleasant way to travel coupled with a short travelling time had given it all the hallmarks of a winner … so far. At least it would have been unusual … anywhere else.

Erina Darklight drew back from where her face had been glued to the small window next to her seat.

'Ah, drat, there went the view,' she grumbled as the Court was replaced by the outer edges of the shiport.

Many of her fellow passengers were still straining to see what was happening on the ground far below, trying to catch a glimpse of where they were going later in the day.

'No worries. I'll see it up close and personal a bit later,'

Erina said. Having lost sight of the Court, Erina's interests now switched to more practical things, like *not* chopping off any nearby heads. The staff with their polite 'excuse me sir, pardon me madam,' were grating on her nerves.

They kept asking her if she needed any assistance. It wasn't like it was the first time she'd been to a shiport or even a spaceport. Hadn't they realised this by now?

She growled under her breath.

Maybe it was the clothes? It was true, you did dress differently when you lived in a Valley all by yourself, but she'd made a point of changing before catching this flight.

Now, Erina pulled on the black jacket she'd kept rolled up behind her neck as a pillow.

It didn't look much like armour — just sharply cut cloth. It felt like armour though. And was it her imagination or did it make those around her edge away just a little?

She hadn't worn anything with the old insignia since first crashing in the Valley. She'd almost forgotten how handy it was. It probably wouldn't win her any races though, Erina thought. For starters, it wouldn't grant anyone more legs or increased speed or any kind of superpowers.

'Too bad. I could have done with a few of those,' she murmured. 'Instant not-sword wielding skills for instance.'

Erina sucked at the finger where she'd cut herself during practice and settled back, choosing to immerse herself in the information on next week's races floating up from her diom. This whole equine business was still new to her and there was much to learn.

Around her, her fellow passengers were wiggling in their seats (well, some of the more excitable ones were). The main track might no longer be visible, but the grounds belonging to the Court — now that was a different story.

They weren't located outside the shiport. If anything, as large as the travel hub was, it was a speck in a sea of green, grey, orange and a myriad of other colours known to nature. Lakes, streams, some minor mountains, even part of the distant ocean, it was all part of the "race track."

'To say that the grounds are extensive would be belittling their true size,' Erina read out loud. 'Hah! It's still smaller than the Valley,' she snorted.

Even those with personal dioms were, if only for the moment, pressing their noses against the transparent plates and pointing. Sure, dioms were great, but there was just something about seeing a race in person that just couldn't be explained; an excitement in the blood that just wouldn't go away and kept them at the edge of their seats even before they'd gotten anywhere near the track itself. Maybe they'd even be lucky, and one would run right next to the local transport shuttle.

'I suppose if you wanted to build something like this from scratch, you could do worse,' Erina mused out loud.

She hoisted up her bag from beneath her feet and put it on the empty seat next to her. The man who'd sat there had gotten off at the last stop — praise be. He'd been regaling her with all sorts of details about his exploits until it had felt like her ears were about to explode. In turn, she'd been amusing herself with imagining feeding him to the local wildlife.

'Going down to see the big leaguers, missy?'

"Missy." That was even worse than "Madame." A frown narrowed her eyes into thin slits.

'Ah, come on! Sure you are. You got the program and all.'

Pointedly ignoring the voices from behind — it wasn't any of her business after all — Erina crossed her arms.

'What's taking so long getting this bucket of bolts on the ground,' she muttered under her breath. 'What is the captain doing? Taking the scenic route?'

Indeed, that *was* exactly what the leafflyer's pilot was doing. It was part of the package — showing off to the new arrivals just how great Epsilon Court really was. Most of them were, after all, here for the races.

That was why the Court had been built in the first place: to feed the latest craze in the racing circuits and it was built to purpose too.

The shiport, which they'd nearly completed a circle around while coming in for landing, was just as new, shiny walls and all. Sometimes the plotted course of a graded race took the whole set of participants *through* parts of the shiport itself.

Erina sighed and folded the information pack she'd received earlier and with which she had been passing the time with on the rather uneventful flight. It folded squarely and then just sat on her knees much like a somewhat passive lapdog. And if she lacked the energy to even put it away properly, she at least resisted any urge to pat it on its non-existent head.

The young woman sat back, only half paying attention to the droning voice reminding all passengers to prepare for landing and to please remember not to forget to leave any small items of questionable value and use behind when disembarking.[2]

She smiled somewhat amusedly. There was something wonderfully incoherent about the whole thing, but that was humans for you. No one ever suggested that they'd make sense or be sensible either for that matter. No wonder her palms began to itch every time she had to spend too long in their company.

They were wonderfully inconsistent creatures, she thought. In a way, it

---

[2] Collecting lost trinkets was a competitive pastime and some collectors saw no harm in asking others to help — all completely voluntarily of course.

was part of their charm — when observed from a distance — but it could get a bit annoying, like an especially large dose of cough medicine. It reminded you that you were human. Erina wondered if they simply up and forgot if they didn't get confirmation on that every five minutes. But perhaps it was more of a question of perspective and *she* was the odd one out. She couldn't say that that thought hadn't occurred to her — sometimes several times a day — as she moved through a world filled with them.

Actually, now, as so many times before, when she thought about it, that was probably the easier explanation, rather than thinking that an entire solar system filled with human beings still lacked somewhat in the ability to find someone sensible. Easier perhaps, but she still preferred the first version. Maybe because it was less depressing.

There was probably some silly universal law about the whole thing.[3]

The building of the Court shouldn't really have come as a surprise though, not when you sat down and had a good, long think about it. Almost everything seemed to move in cycles and, after all, they raced just about everything else that could be ridden on, in, behind, or — in one case — in front, so why not horses?

Of course, around here, that might not always mean what you thought it meant. Here, a horse could be so much more...

Admittedly, *most* of the things that were being raced had an engine of metal and wires and tended to go "vroom" "vroom" "wwrroooom!" rather than "neigh," but natural racing had seen a growing comeback during the last few years. If you went in person, you could actually see the racers for more than point zero four seconds at a time as they streaked past. And you didn't need to struggle into a spacesuit either or worry about running out of oxygen from shouting yourself hoarse when your favourite was about to cross the finish line twenty thousand kilometres away.

No matter how impressive the interplanetary ships and speeders were, no matter how sleek or shiny, they were a bit too fast to catch more than a glimpse of when they weren't standing still or merely lazing about. That was the point of them after all. It just didn't make for a very exciting first person

---

[3] Universal Narrative Imperative, subclause b — maybe.

perspective.

They were also darn hard to make out against a backdrop of infinite space and when you hit an asteroid at full speed (because you'd rerouted the power from the anti-collision system to your boosters because that asshat from Friga was catching you up); you probably weren't going to shake that off with an aspirin and a stiff drink and then go back and do the same thing again tomorrow.

There, the natural races were way ahead of the game. Except in the saddest cases, accidents rarely resulted in a shower of sparks, a loud bang, and a small crater where competitor and/or audience had been merely moments before. Though, with some mounts, you might run the risk of being eaten if you fell off.

Keen followers of the mechanized races thought that the naturals were slow, boring, and, at the end of the day, not about *you*, the person in charge.

'Who wants to be *half* of a bloody team?' they'd snort. 'You're not even out there making your own decision. So what, if your ride throws a hissy fit and refuses to play ball.'

At which point someone in their audience, provided they weren't all die-hard mechanized racing fans that is, would let slip 'Oh yeah, and the bloody machines always do what you tell them, right?'

The name 'Johnny' would most likely be snickered somewhere in the background before more laughter erupted and the gathering broke up (or got violent).

Someone at her old workplace had once suggested she'd enter and make a name for herself.

'Yeah, sure,' Erina had growled at them at the time. 'That's a great idea. Why don't we power up the engines, set fire to this old rustbucket and leap into the nearest supersized black hole while we're at this, eh?'

Erina had never met the man — nor did she want to emulate him — but even she had *heard* of him. The last time one of the crew had pestered her about it, she'd nailed one of the engineers to the outer hull with his own gun. It was a good thing for him they'd been parked at the docks at the time.

Indeed, there was not one on-board the *Random Star* who'd failed to remember Johnny Logan and the Amazing Circle of Fire a couple of years back.

One of the one-man ships in the Asteroid Circuit had blown a fuse[4] mid-race and had been going round and round in ever tighter circles, effectively chasing its own tail, had it had one, all while the pilot had been heard over the prime broadcast screaming at it to stop.

He might have been hitting it with something at that point, though those sounds *could* have been the hull banging into random bits of debris.

In the end, they'd only managed to bring him back in because the main power crystals had developed a crack and effectively gone "poof."

It had *not* been one of the pilot's greater triumphs. It was, however, undoubtedly the best remembered bit of racing trivia out of his entire career, much to his displeasure.

'No,' the natural racing fans told anyone who cared to listen. 'If you fell off a horse all you had to worry about were the few feet to the ground and any hooves in the vicinity.'

Unless you were in a canyon or such, in which case the drop might be a teensy weensy bit more inconvenient. Or you were riding something just a wee bit bigger than a horse that could squash you flat without even noticing. Or it was a nightmare you had just gotten thrown from, in which case you should probably have been starting counting your body parts even "before" the moment you lost your seat. Or... or...

No, what you didn't need to worry about was the distinct lack of the presence of vacuum. Or lack of presence, seeing as vacuum implied that there wasn't anything in it, which it, being space, there most certainly was: dust, radio waves, and stuff to start with and working its way up to planetoids and suns at the other end of the spectrum.

The reason you worried was because it had suddenly appeared, where hitherto no vacuum had been, on account of you just having parted company with your stellar racer.

Of course, that whole thing would be countered with an, 'Oh yeah? You guys fly too you know. Not so fun when your ride drops dead five miles up in the air, is it chummy?'

---

[4] Or whatever it was that those ship thingies did anyway. Most people's eyes started to glaze over before the mechanics had even begun warming to their topic

To everyone not following the life of racing, listening to either of the parties was as much fun as listening to two old professors set in their ways arguing about the notorious chicken and the egg story or some local equivalent. At which point said listeners would usually give up and go and do something more constructive with their time.

Overall though, the two camps got along about as well as could be expected.

Still, natural racing was new (technically speaking it wasn't as much "new" as it was "resurrected," but who was counting) and exciting, and it did have the advantage that you could see it. You could stand right at the fence and smell it. You could feel the wind in your own face just as much as those people coming around the bend "over there" did. It was "up close and personal" in almost every sense of the word; that was the main selling point, according to their promoters anyway. At least, it was if you were one of those standing at that first row of the fence. It was a somewhat more detached affair up in the bleachers.

Erina leaned back, closing her eyes while "landing" happened all around her, and wondered what in the world she'd gotten herself into.

'Not like I *need* to socialize. The Valley's got plenty for me to do. Got to finish that new stable before winter, too.'

But here she was. At the Epsilon Court, one of the most unusual circuits to have ever been built. It certainly wasn't in search of a good conversation — Erina could give a clam a run for its money (though it'd be a very strange mollusc to be using currency of any kind). What did she have to prove? She wasn't sure — there was just this deep drive to do *something*.

'Excuse me? Madam? We're docked now, madam.'

Erina was brought out of her thoughts by an increasingly insistent steward who kept reminding her that it was time to disembark and could she please remember to collect any belongings before she left the craft.

She shuddered. Promising herself that the next person who called her "madam" would be strung up by their toenails, she gathered up her belongings and made her way off the leafflyer.

Looking around, Erina could see the hastily retreating backs of a few of her fellow stragglers and, after realizing she wasn't sure where to go, growled a low 'bugger' and made her escape into the building beyond.

The terminal itself was, as you would have expected, filled with people milling about with various degrees of determination. It was also full of the kind of things that spring up wherever large numbers of people gather: tables, small chairs, relaxing miniature waterfalls, small forests of pot plants, an *actual* forest, things like that.

What it didn't contain were any signs. There were lots and lots of floor space, but no arrows or little green pointers to where you could find x, y, or z.

Well, supposedly it contained an equal amount of ceiling space as well but, since no one was trying to walk on that it didn't really count. Okay, it had walls too — though a lot of those also doubled as windows. The overall effect was a bit like walking around inside a giant and very open-planned greenhouse except it wasn't boiling hot or humid and distinctly devoid of insects buzzing around and trying to nest in your ears.

At the moment, there were even more people around than usual, creating a hustling and bustling crowd moving at what seemed to very often be complete cross purposes.

That was to be expected. It was a main shiport's terminal after all and with the Phoenix Stakes coming up in the next week, the influx of visitors to the area was increasing accordingly; the Phoenix Stakes being a popular event to visit in person as much for a relaxing few days out as it was for the competition itself.

No matter how gratifying the increased number of human bodies was for the locals, the throng of people was making it difficult to see where she was going.

'Excuse me!' Erina swivelled around to glare at several autonomous pieces of luggage. 'That was my *foot*!'

The three large suitcases whistled and tried to swerve around her. She moved in front of them.

'Oh no you don't! Where's your owner? Didn't he teach you *any* manners?'

They beeped at her in unison, the sound of annoyed vehicles when you were hogging their lane and they were in a hurry.

'Yeah? You too!' Erina nearly waved her fist at them as they split up, passed her on the side, and sped down the walkway. 'Great, now I'm yelling at machines.' She took a deep breath and hoisted her bag back over her shoulder.

'Too bad those won't run in the Valley,' she muttered to herself. 'It would have been handy not having to do every bit of lifting and carrying around the place myself.'

Erina sighed. 'That's what you get for living in a place where electricity refuse to work, I guess.'

Increasingly grim-faced, her eyes darted between the directions from the diom and the world around her. Thanks to it, she was at least not going to get lost. Not completely anyway. It didn't stop her feet wandering off in the wrong direction when she got distracted.

On the other hand, navigating a huge, milling crowd, all individual parts straining and pulling, fully intent on their own journeys and worries, was tricky even at optimal circumstances. For a small, slender female of less than average height, it left a great deal to be desired.

She never had liked crowds. Except to hide in.

It was a good thing that most of the people in this place were, mostly, good-natured — if somewhat excitable — rather than hostile. Pushing and shoving was kept to a minimum. In turn, slicing and dicing was also off the board.

Erina sighed. 'Next time, I fly *all* the way,' she said. 'On my own ship. I should get one parked outside the Valley — too bad you never really know where you're gonna come out when you leave that place.'

Even one of those private pick-up services sounded really good right about now. One of the many she'd seen advertised in the info pack she'd received when registering for the Phoenix Stakes. She was beginning to wish she'd used one of them rather than insisting on making her own way down. Still, old habits die hard — or so they said — and she really loathed being dependent on others.

'Hup, hup.' Clutching her backpack closer, Erina slipped past a laughing group of people all dressed in various shades of green.

Beyond them, she glimpsed one of the many entryways to the complex.

'Right, now all I need to do is to find some sort of local transport and I'm all sorted. Do I know where I'm going?' she slapped her pocket with her note. 'Yes, I do. Onwards and upwards then.'

The young woman made a face. She had never liked visiting places like these, not even in her old job, and she definitely didn't like visiting them for the first time.

She preferred doing so when it was dark. It felt more comfortable, more *right*, somehow. In the shadows, there was a way to relax that the suns never brought out. You felt one with the night.

It also mean people were less likely to see you.

Standing, alone, high-above, surveying everything from tall buildings and stocky farmhouses to wide plains of verdant dunes, it was peaceful. Not unlike the calm before the storm, but a storm where you chose when it should rain down.

Once outside and away from the crowds — she'd never learn to like those, not in a million years —t it proved easy enough to flag down a transporter for Epsilon Court. There were several around and there were plenty of people getting in and out of them.

Erina noted that she'd managed to get hold of one without wheels. That was nice. Wheels made for an uncomfortable, often bumpy, journey and had been going out of fashion for some time. Though they persisted in some regions and they did have their uses, she quickly realized why there were so few around the shiport; there were no roads.

Guess it made sense when you thought about it. The consortium behind the newly modelled "Court" was widely known to be one of the main powers behind the current drive of 'ecolizing.'

Ecolizing was all well and good in Erina's books, but, if anyone had bothered to ask, which of course they never did, she thought it would have been better not to have messed things up in the first place.

Though, if she had to be honest, there was an awful lot of planet and a fairly limited amount of mess. Most of the world was pretty much the same as it had been when people first settled here (okay, crashed here). That was changing though — but not in ways that a casual observer from the great beyond might have expected.

Whatever the truth behind the first landing was, it hadn't been anywhere near catastrophic enough to knock the rather unexpected pioneers back into the Stone Age, which was something to be thankful for at least. Erina liked her technology — she just wanted it to be unobtrusive and, even better, unseen.

Not that any of it made any difference when you got right down to it. Whatever the reason behind it, the important part, in her mind, was that they *had* arrived.

Erina brushed a few non-existent specks of dust from her black trousers while staring at the passing scenery through pale, round windows.

So boring, she thought. Tired or not, Erina loathed being bored. She beat out a popular rhythm with her fingers. Tap. Tap. Tappity. Tap. Tap.

Nope. Still bored… Weren't they there yet?

They entered into a cloud of dust. Soon after, Erina caught sight of a wild looking gaggle of animals and riders up ahead. As they passed them, some strained to race the machine only to fall behind as the leader — a sleek grey creature, snaked out his head and tried to bite them. White fangs flashed outside the window. Then the transport pulled ahead.

'Coming in for the Stakes, miss?' the driver asked casually as he skilfully manoeuvred the small transporter around a maxima grinding to a halt before them.

'After a fashion,' Erina admitted.

'It's getting mighty popular. They're having a big fireworks festival to mark the end of it this year. That should be something to see,' the driver said.

'Mhm…'

She wished he'd be quiet, but instead he kept up a happy banter all the way to the central complex of the Court. Erina's contributions to the conversation could easily be summed up as an occasional grunt or distracted nod. This didn't seem to faze him at all.

The transporter eventually dropped her off outside the main check-in office for the Court. From there it'd be easy to find her way once she'd gotten the arrival registrations sorted — she hoped.

'Stupid paperwork,' Erina grumbled while pushing open the glass doors to the main atrium.

Still, once she'd gotten this done and dropped off her stuff, she could go and see how Harlan was doing. That bit was the only part of the day she'd been looking forward to. Erina hadn't been all that fond of having to send her companion ahead. She hoped he was doing well.

She imagined he did. Harlan Illusion was a horse and a half and as long as they'd found someone to fuss over him and let him run free, he'd be happy.

'How do I get to this place from here?' Erina asked the person behind the desk, pointing at the map on her diom.

The registration had gone quicker than she'd expected and she was eager to both see her four-legged friend and to get some sleep.

'You'll have to take the long way around, I'm afraid. There's an internal shuttle every twenty minutes.'

'Great. When's the next one?'

'Twenty minutes. Sorry, you just missed it.'

'Splendid!' Erina didn't even bother to keep the sarcasm out of her voice. 'And why do I have to take the "long way around" anyway?'

'Oh — you don't know? It's the nightmares.'

This revelation earned little more than a shrug as Erina threw her backpack over her shoulder.

'Miss. Wait, miss, you can't go that way!' the receptionist called after her as Erina walked out and headed towards where Harlan was stabled as the crow flies. 'That's the nightmares there. Aren't you worried about the *nightmares*?'

Erina treated the other woman to a mirthless grin over her shoulder. 'Oh, I don't scare so easily.'

CHAPTER TWO

The immediate area around the central complex was busy, but as Erina kept walking, the sight of horses being walked on leads and automated wheelbarrows trundling over the uneven ground began to give way to high durasteel fences.

Instead of jaunty caps, people here wore headgear that wouldn't have looked out of place at a stampede of volcanoes.

There were far less people about too. And instead of one person to a horse, the ones she caught sight of in the distance were surrounded by up to four people at once.

In light of that, the music streaming from a passing open door, while perfectly ordinary, felt out of place, like a clown showing up at a funeral.

Erina kept one eye on her diom — which was pointing steadily north — and one on her surroundings. She still jumped when there came an almighty crash from the direction of the stables, followed by a lot of people shouting: 'He's loose! He's loose!'

Calls of, 'Out of the way!' 'After him!' and, 'Watch out!' followed the sounds of semblance-wood being turned into matchsticks. The walls of the building shook from the impact of something … big.

Part of the façade shattered as a large animal barrelled through it trailing ropes and steel lines. It shook a heavy head — as if the impact had dazed it no matter how thick its skull was.

It bellowed and heaved itself back on its four, hooved feet, kicking another hole in the wall behind it while it did so.

Small, blueish eyes rolled and, with a buck, the beast was off, thundering down the pathway into the open ground. As it hit another, smaller fence, its pursuers rounded the corner of the stable building.

Bellowing gutturally, the remains of the saddle caught momentarily on the fencepost. It barely noticed, continuing to barrel forwards. With high durasteel fences on either side, the main pathway was really the only way it could go.

'Go! Get out of the way!' someone shouted at her from far away.

Erina looked about. Unless someone suggested she'd suddenly grow wings and fly out, there wasn't really any place for her *to* go.

Her eyes narrowed as the riding-beast approached, its powerful hooves gouging holes in the dirt path.

'Don't even think about it buddy,' she muttered darkly under her breath as her muscles tensed.

The animal, easily twice her height and nearly as broad, swerved around her.

'Well, wasn't that exciting,' Erina said casually.

'Miss? Everything alright, miss?' some of the pursuers stopped (possibly to catch their breath if anything) by her.

'Of course. Shouldn't they be?' Erina asked.

Apparently, this wasn't the response they expected, because she could see confusion sideswiping their faces.

'Well, um … this is kind of a restricted area.'

'Really? It doesn't look that way to me,' Erina said cooly, pointing her thumb after the escaping beast. 'Maybe you should catch it before it gets even further away?' she suggested when the three men seemed reluctant to leave.

Deciding that their escapee was more important than some random human, they all set off after it.

'So, that was a nightmare, was it? Guess it takes all sorts,' Erina said to herself. 'They'd probably have more luck if they called in for some air support. Do they think they'll run that thing down on foot? Ha!'

By the time Erina crossed into more normal equine territory, she'd seen several nightmares — some even up close. Not two looked the same.

This new section of stable wasn't nearly as vast. It also faced outwards.

Unlike the nightmare's buildings which, at most, had small, round windows near the roof, here she was faced with row upon row of open-faced loose-boxes.

Birch, maple, and other natural woods had been the inspiration here — creating the sensation that you hadn't just walked into the output of a whole semblance-tree factory, but back in time too.

'Great,' Erina sighed. 'As if I didn't get enough of trees at home.'

The open top of the loose box didn't reveal much, mostly just a deep shadow, the "sun"[5] being on the other side of the sky.

Of course, standing in said sunlight and looking in didn't help. As she passed them by, the crunch of her boots against the ground brought out several shapely heads.

'Curious fellows, aren't you?' Erina mumbled as she kept on walking and more and more heads popped up. 'Well, at least it's easy to see which boxes are occupied.'

It wasn't just her they were interested in. Closer to where the building made a sort of L-turn, there was a new arrival being led into the stable, and it had roused a lot of curiosity and a fair bit of rivalry from some of the closer neighbours.

Standing on tiptoe she peeked into an empty stall. The inside walls were a uniform eggshell white with details in a pale, but warm, blue-green that, despite their distinct wooden appearance, made her feel like she'd just stuck her head into a fishbowl.

It looked remarkably non-dusty. The small stable back home in the Valley collected dust like nobody's business. Not to mention random straws, bits of leaves and, one time, a dead vole stuffed into a hole.

'That's modern technology for you, I guess,' Erina said. 'I really could do with something like this. It'd save a lot of time.' Which could then be spent on other work instead. Maybe she was crazy for trying to build something up from scratch all by herself? No, Erina shook her head. 'You knew it was going to take time when you decided to do this,' she told herself. 'No point in getting

---

[5] Suns if you wanted to be picky about it. Though why only one of them was shining when you were down on a planet when they clearly were hanging there in space like overinflated gasbags, was anyone's guess.

cold feet now.'

There were a number of people around the yard that these boxes lined — none of whom were paying much attention to her. Or "seemed" not to be paying attention. She doubted many of them were quite as oblivious as they pretended.

Wondering if the one she'd come to see was out at the moment, Erina stuck her head over yet another bar door. Leaning in, she smiled. Finally, an occupant she recognized.

Erina unlatched the lower door and slipped inside.

'There you are, hmm? What'cha doing in here? Shouldn't you be out running around somewhere right about now?' she quipped lightly.

At the sound of her voice, the horse stopped trying to excavate the bottom of his feed tray and shuffled around, happily sticking his head under her left arm.

'Easy there,' Erina chided laughingly as the muscled neck made her stumble backwards. 'I'm not a block of concrete you know.'

She rubbed Harlan affectionately between the eyes.

Then she noticed, even in the shadow of the box, odd bits of pale yellow against the black and white of the horse's mane and tail. A gentle tugging at these proved them to be bits of bedding.

'What have you been up to, you naughty boy?'

She waved the bits of straw under the white muzzle and Harlan lipped lazily after them.

'And here I thought horses were supposed to sleep standing up,' she patted his neck, 'not carousing around like a mad Duke of Fornburn. It would appear that I was wrong,' Erina chuckled.

'Well, let's see about giving you a good onceover, shall we? I'm sure they've put the brushes around here somewhere … and a lead. I did pack one for you, you know.'

To the sounds of the yard were now added the random mutterings of a young woman starting to search through the nooks and crannies for the lead rope she was sure had been there but a moment earlier.

After a while they were replaced by an exasperated sigh as Erina turned around. Hands on her hips she gave her horse an accusing eyeful.

'Harlan, what have I told you about playing "silly buggers" with me? Did *you* move it when I wasn't looking?'

The red, white, and black trias offered nothing but an innocent expression and instead tried begging for a treat. This usually worked. But today, his human was unusually persistent.

'Not now boy,' Erina gently pushed the inquisitive muzzle out of the way. 'Be a good fella and find the lead, won't you?' she asked. 'Since you probably was the one who stole it.'

Harlan merely swished his tail to dislodge a couple of flies.

Anyone that *might* have been casually eavesdropping just out of sight, found themselves wondering if the young stranger really expected the horse to answer. Hopefully she was simply filling in that end of the conversation in her head — as so many people did — though perhaps not quite so vocally.

Possibly that was because it made them sound silly, Seranthiem thought as he paused outside the stable doors. *He'd* never do anything like that. Well, at least not when he was likely to be overheard anyway.

A gentle crease graced his forehead for but a moment. 'This could prove quite burdensome,' he said softly.

Seranthiem wasn't sure which was the greater concern: working with owners who were somewhat "unusual" in their tastes and mannerisms was common enough — and he appeared to have a knack for being assigned to them, much to his detriment. But working for one that was possibly slightly deranged was another matter entirely.

At times like these, it would be best to take a cautionary approach, he thought to himself.

'Remember why you took this job.' Seranthiem shuddered involuntarily and, as the memory rose, he pushed down hard. Like an iceberg cork, it always rose again from the bottom of his deepest self, but still, he tried.

Maybe he should go introduce himself instead of standing here and dredging up unpleasant, old memories?

There was also the possibility that this *wasn't* the horse's owner. He'd been assigned to the horse only a week or so before, by the board. That was common enough. Most entrants to the Stakes arrived in stages over time — especially those who came from far afield, and all but the most driven didn't send an entourage of staff along with the animals in question.

That did mean he'd never actually met the woman … girl? He doubted there was any cause for concern. While she didn't look much like her picture, which had given the perception of a stern, unapproachable figure, there was another factor in her favour; Harlan didn't protest her presence. If anything, the painted horse was as excited as a kitten having just found a ball of string but was too aware of his size to act on it.

Still, while he might be relatively new to this type of work (hence why he'd been assigned to a new, lower ranking stable such as High Fyelds in the first place), he took his duties seriously enough.

'Ahem!' Seranthiem cleared his throat.

This didn't seem to induce any kind of response from the inside.

'Excuse me,' he said, louder this time. 'May I ask, who might you be?'

'Aha! There you are! Bad rope!' Erina scolded the lead she'd just discovered hiding under the hay.

'Excuse me!' Seranthiem raised his voice. 'Hello!'

Straightening up and flinging the lead over her shoulder, Erina turned and finally appeared to notice the presence at the door.

'Oh, hi. Who are you?' she asked, cocking her head slightly to the right as she did so.

'Perhaps you could begin with letting *me* know who you are first?' Seranthiem insisted pointedly. He tried to keep any irritation he felt out of his voice. He was good at that — usually. But today just seemed to be one of those days.

'Should I?' Erina responded, her eyes narrowing.

She didn't bother to wait for an answer but took the opportunity to clip on the newfound lead to the black leather halter that Harlan was wearing. Apparently, they'd seen fit to replace the perfectly serviceable one made of hemp rope that she'd been using.

Even in the semi-shadow of the box, deeper now that he was blocking some of the sunlight, Seranthiem could tell that she was frowning. Was she lurking in the shadows on purpose, to keep him confused? If so, it was in vain. He had keen eyes, sharper than most in fact. A little tidbit of unusualness he rarely shared with anyone.

'I do believe so, yes,' he instead retorted calmly.

'Oh, right,' Erina said with a shrug.

There didn't follow anything immediately after that. Did she mean to not answer after all? The moment of silence stretched out, making him wonder if he should take the initiative yet again.

'Erina. Erina Darklight. And in case it somehow escaped your notice … my name's on the door!'

Hard, amber eyes stared him down as the words flowed over him like a gladiatorial challenge. He wondered what would happen to someone who took her up on that?

'Yes, so it is,' Seranthiem agreed pleasantly, pretending he didn't notice her tone. 'But perhaps it would be prudent to also be able to prove it?'

He took a moment to have a good look at the person he was talking to.

She was younger than he had expected. A lot younger. When first reading the instructions on this assignment, he'd developed this image of a matronly, but distinguished, lady who'd spent a lifetime amassing knowledge and sarcasm in equal proportion. The type who would probably collect things and leave them about the house and stable alike, drape hand-knitted rugs over every surface, and keep cats.

Despite the photo attached, that vision had kept drifting back. Now he could feel it shatter like a broken mirror. He *could* imagine this lady keeping cats. But the fluffy Persians he'd pictured, turned into roaring, sabre-toothed tigers before his eyes.

'Well, I could get Harlie to bite your head off,' Erina suggested sweetly. 'Would that qualify? Who are you anyway?'

No, instead of a slightly batty, old lady, what he seemed to have gotten was a youngish woman of indeterminable age, with curly, dark blond hair reaching just below her shoulders and an attitude that could switch at the drop of a stun gun. He'd been right about the "small" part though. And the sarcasm.

A bare trace of distaste passed over his features as Seranthiem winced at her choice of introduction. 'I deserved that, perhaps,' he said, happy he managed to resist the urge to say something far less polite.

'I'm not at my best at the moment,' he said instead. 'My apologies. I am your assigned caretaker. My name is Seranthiem.'

'Forty hours without any sleep and the same goes for me, Sam,' Erina admitted and pushed some hair out of her eyes. It immediately fell back again.

'Seranthiem.'

'Does anyone actually call you that?' Erina wondered, thinking back on how many people on-board the *Random Star* had been known by shorthand or even nicknames. When you'd just misstepped and started to drift away from the satellite you were supposed to be working on, you wanted something short and easy to remember to yell into the coms.

'Usually,' he replied.

'How curious,' Erina said. 'How are you with being called Sam?'

'I'll survive,' Seranthiem held back a sigh. He was having the strangest feeling he was going to be losing a lot of arguments in the near future.

'Great,' Erina said and turned her attention back to Harlan who was standing patiently but with every inch of his body saying he wanted to be doing something exciting, not listen to them making odd noises at each other. 'Come on fella, let's get you all nice and groomed, shall we?'

Harlan followed obediently, pausing only for a moment to try and munch at a stray bit of hair in what would pass as an affectionate way.

Sam closed the lower door behind them, hating to leave things untidy.

Erina blinked in the sudden sunlight. Her eyes constricted both from lack of sleep and effort to see the person she was talking to. He'd been standing right in the light, so, until now, all she'd gotten was a very tall, willowy outline.

'If you do not mind me saying so, why did you not go get some rest before coming here,' Sam wondered curiously as Erina sleepily searched for somewhere they wouldn't be in the way.

She shrugged. 'It's only early afternoon here. I'd end up waking up in the middle of night thinking it was time to get up if I did that,' she said, stifling a yawn. 'These planetary time shifts always mess me up. Besides, I wanted to see if everything was alright. I didn't want Harlie coming here on his own in the first place, but it was either a question of grabbing the spot when it turned up or wait another year. I was lucky to get offered it in the first place. Just plain bad timing that I'd be off-world at the time.'

'Naturally,' Seranthiem agreed.

'Perhaps you could make yourself useful and find some brushes,' Erina suggested.

'Yes, of course. I have some in my locker. Items like brushes and similar tend to lead a somewhat mobile life here.'

'That'd be nice,' Erina replied as she dropped the lead rope on the ground.

I wouldn't do that, Seranthiem thought. The horse will walk away from her. Should I tell her? 'I'll go fetch them then, shall I?' he asked instead. 'It will take but a moment.'

For some reason, Sam felt a need to retreat from the situation until he could get a hold on what was happening and hurried into the stable proper to retrieve the errant brushes. This left behind a somewhat grim-faced, young woman.

'Well, that was odd,' Erina commented to her horse.

The bright red, black, and white Harlan didn't reply. How could he? She patted him affectionately. Harlan and Mordjen were great company, but no matter how much she valued her privacy, some actual conversation now and then wouldn't hurt.

They had a bit of time to themselves at last it seemed. Erina closed her eyes, leaning forward with her arms around Harlan's muscular neck. For a while, she just stood there, breathing in the familiar scent.

Normally, he smelled of the wilds, endless grasslands and dense forests — now that was mixed with something far more civilized. Erina wasn't sure she liked it.

But it was a bit of quiet, away from everything else. Like so many other times of quiet, it didn't last very long.

'Eh, miss? Miss? Excuse me, miss!'

Erina eventually realized that someone was talking to her and raised a curious eyebrow in the direction of the speaker. 'Yes?' she said politely, if somewhat confused. 'Can I help you?'

'Everything alright?'

'Yes, quite shipshape,' Erina replied bluntly.

She blinked a couple of times, trying to gather her thoughts. She kept looking at the old man standing before her, suddenly feeling disorganized and muddled through and through.

'Shouldn't I be?' she wondered after a short pause.

'I was just wondering, see. That horse can be difficult,' the man retorted casually. 'Though I see you've got him nice and docile.' He chuckled. 'I've seen him on the practices, I have. He sure is an energetic one that one. Zigging and zagging all over the place.'

A small scowl caressed Erina's brow. 'I'm sorry, sir, I don't think I caught your name?' she asked a bit more pointedly than she'd intended.

'Probably 'cause I didn't give it!' The old man grinned disarmingly and thrust out a hand in her general direction.

Tufts of his white hair bounced in the breeze. Erina tried not to notice the way it moved though. After the long journey, she hadn't settled down physically yet, earthbound travel always took a lot out of her, and the way the hair kept jumping around was slowly threatening to make her seasick. Too bad it did its best to draw every bit of attention to it.

'Castle's the name. Jim Castle.' He shook her hand enthusiastically. 'I'm seeing to the left wing.'

Left wing of what? Erina wondered, though she kept that thought to herself. 'Erina Darklight. Pleased to meet you,' she said instead.

'Darklight, eh? That's quite an unusual name you've got there. Don't see many of those around anymore,' the old man said. He pulled thoughtfully at the wisp of beard that clung half-heartedly to his chin. 'Not related to Erasmus Darklight, the inventor of the two-way climaxing T engine revolver, are you?' he queried, peering at her good-naturedly.

'Err ... sorry?' Erina tried to gather what few wits she still had left over from being awake too long. 'Umm ... I don't think so...' she hesitated before continuing. 'Who was he?'

'I suppose he was a *bit* before your time,' Castle admitted.

Erina tugged at her hand, which the old man was still pumping up and down absentmindedly. She really would like it back right about now, she thought.

'Sorry, could you...' she pulled a bit harder, indicating that she'd *really* like it back, thank you very much.

Castle looked down, as if he was seeing both their hands for the first time.

'Oh, sorry about that. Forget my old head next,' he declared loftily.

'So, what do you do around here?' Erina asked, having feverishly cast around for something to say. If she'd had it her way, it'd be a fist in the nose, but that was generally frowned upon.

'Told ye already. I look after the West Wing. The *whole* West Wing — and that's no easy job, I tell ya. Don't ever let anyone tell ya that it's an easy job.' Castle pulled at his nose, obviously warming to his subject.

'Oh, these guys think they've got it tough with all these high-strung prima donnas prancing about all over the place. But let me tell you…' he shook his head. 'Sure, they worry they might get into a fight and get a scratch. Bless. Us, we worry if this is the day ye get yer arm torn off. At least none of their charges tries to eat the others.' Castle snorted.

'Umm…'

'Of course, I've got things to distract me,' Castle chuckled, waving the thick book he'd been holding in his other hand, under her nose.

'Yes, I see.'

'Want to have a look?'

'Look? Look at what?' There was a slight trace of panic in her voice as Erina's eyes darted about seeking an escape.

'What d'ya think girlie? *This*!' Castle gave the book another wave.

'What? Oh, the book. Right.'

Erina gingerly took hold of the thick volume with about the same enthusiasm as someone picking up a poisonous snake. Carefully, one eye on the book and another one on Jim, and yet another one on Harlan (though this was a difficult feat since she only had two of them), she read the title.

'Experimental Field Theories: Quasi Dimensional Engineering and its Role in Society,' she read out loud.

Erina read it again, just in case it would make more sense the second time around. It didn't. She could understand every single word in the sentence. She just had absolutely no idea what the sentence itself was actually supposed to mean.

Erina turned the book over in case that could shed some light on the matter.

'Not really my field I'm afraid,' she confessed. 'The only thing I know is that QDE is what enables the power stations to be built and anything and everything that run on internal power as well.'

She frowned again as she gave that another thought. 'Actually, I don't really *know* that either. It's what everyone learns. It's supposedly the basis of society as we know it.'

'Oh, that it does girlie. That it does,' Castle agreed knowingly and accepted the book back. 'Some day, it'll even bring us back out among the stars, ya'll see. None of this skipping around the solar system like some overgrown grasshoppers. *Proper* space travel, I tell you. Not in my time though. Probably not in yours either. But one day … ya'll see,' Castle nodded eagerly and then heaved a small sigh.

'Still, we do what we can to help out. I lecture up at the university at times. Think I might even have a professorship somewhere. Though I'll be damned if I remember where.'

'Yes, well, very nice. Must make a nice contrast to this place,' Erina murmured quietly, something spiky edging its way into her voice.

'Less than ya'd think girlie. Less than ya think,' Castle chuckled again. 'Anyway, I see young Semmie's coming. Better be off. He's a nice enough young fella, if somewhat odd. See ya around miss.'

And with those last words, he gave a small wave and vanished among the rest of the buildings.

'Yes, see ya — eh, no, you, around,' Erina gazed grimly at where the old man had disappeared beyond a handy corner. 'Preferably long-distance,' she added when she was sure he was out of hearing range.

Erina sighed, annoyed with herself. She'd spent so much time shut away up at High Fyelds recently that she'd completely forgotten what it was like "down here" or so it felt. Apparently, interpersonal skills were something that you needed to practice to keep your hand in.

'Silly really,' she muttered disdainfully. 'I, of anyone, should know better than to judge by appearances.'

Still didn't keep her from wanting to connect several people's foreheads with the nearest hard surface. That's where self-control came in.

CHAPTER THREE

Entwining her fingers in the horse's long black mane, rolling its white tips between them, Erina rested her head against his side, slowly drawing in the scent of warm horse and hay. It was strangely relaxing, like a little bit of home that was here rather than there. After the last few days in space, she really needed that. To say they'd been hectic would have been the understatement of the ages.

'Odd, really. I never thought I'd think of somewhere so far from, well, *everything* as "home."'

It was true that Erina might not care much for crowds, but she cared even less for things happening on short notice or, even worse, with no notice at all.

Surprises were pretty much lumped into the same category. And Sam had come as a bit of a surprise, no doubt about it. He was *not* what she'd been given to expect from the notifications by the Court's-council.

Admittedly, she hadn't been able to get a very good look at him while in the box; all she had been able to see was a very willow-like shadow against the light. She knew, of course, that the Court's council had provided someone to look after her horse while he was here, but, when thinking about, them she certainly hadn't imagined anyone like *that*!

He sure had beaten a hasty retreat though, she thought. Was she really that scary? It made her smile.

'Strange person,' she mumbled. 'Wonder if everyone else here is like that too?'

She dismissed that idea right away. She might have spent the time waiting for him to come back so far without having a decent look around, but she'd been paying plenty of attention while walking here.

True, she'd been more interested in the security details, possible escape routes, and any potential dangers that might have been lurking around rather than socializing but that didn't mean she'd been blind.

Besides, there was no way she'd be able to tour this place in a single day. There must be much, much more that was waiting to be explored.

That was to be expected. Epsilon Court covered acres upon acres of land. More than some countries back on Old Earth — if she remembered her history right. The various stables and buildings took up minimal space in comparison. Though, when you had to navigate your way through them, the collection of structures seemed almost endless, to say nothing about bewildering in their layout.

On the other hand, maybe that wasn't really all that strange. After all, Epsilon Court was home to far more than just a few mere horse races; the people behind it apparently being firm believers in the old axiom of "maximum amount of output for a minimum amount of input," something Erina could thoroughly agree with.

And so, while the central buildings covered less than one percent of the total land, the different stables contained not only space for various types of competition equines but a whole host of other creatures as well, ranging in size from something like a large Earth rabbit to those towering several meters above the ground, and that was without counting their heads.

Epsilon Court didn't just spread out far and wide. It had expanded into the subterranean as well.

Down below the ordinary stables were several levels where the more mechanically inclined racers lived, including a large number of the ever-popular stingships. The smallest of the stellar racers, a stingship looked a bit like someone had cropped off the first third of a sowing needle and welded on a whole set of engines.

'Why anyone would even want to trust a flying pin is beyond me,' Erina used to mutter every time she saw one. That was back when she still worked on the *Random Star*.

These days, there were a fair few that belonged to people who weren't into racing at all but just wanted an extra speedy way of getting from A to B —

and weren't claustrophobic.

Personally, she preferred a bit more space. A lot more space actually. It was good that, from where she was standing, between two low-slung buildings on the far right, she could see the beginnings of the actual grounds. That put her somewhere on the very outskirts of the central complex.

'Wonder if we could go for a ride out there?' Erina asked Harlan. 'It's certainly big enough and it'd be nice getting away from all this. It's not at all what you imagine when you hear the words "racecourse" is it?'

While there were what others would have termed "flat racing" floating around, it wasn't something that was particularly catered for at Epsilon Court. A lot of people here figured that it lacked somewhat in excitement, much preferring to watch things that went up and down and, if possible, from side to side and in and out as well. In this day and age, it was becoming increasingly popular to test many, many things at once.

Much like a pilot had to be able to do more than just fly in a straight line before he, or she, or it, was awarded their wings; the competitors had to master multiple disciplines if they wanted to achieve victory at the Court.

The favoured challenge was for a competition to be held in a natural environment. Though — if you had to be completely honest about it — there wasn't all that much "naturalness" about the grounds. They'd been created almost entirely from scratch, landscaped even, to look and act, like the real thing. Indeed, they did make a very good impression of pretending it was real and it saved on long hikes into the wilderness.

'Suppose they had to do something with that big smouldering crater,' Erina shrugged. 'QDEs have gotten a lot safer since back then. And you know, this is getting to be a very one-sided conversation you know. They could have done with adding a mountain or two. They could even have had one of mine,' she said, 'it's not like the Valley doesn't have enough of the dratted things.'

If anything, the grounds were a natural environment with a twist, incorporating within its radius everything from flat grasslands and rolling hills, exposed rock formations and tall cliffs. There were several types of forests and woods with goodness knew how many types of trees. Lakes and ponds and streams, even a whole river (albeit not a very big one), and some marshland. A distinctly sandy desert hadn't been landscaped but remained from the original environment.

If it hadn't been missing all those mountains, it would have reminded her a bit of home. But here, wherever direction she faced, there was a blue horizon in the far distance.

The collection of buildings that made up the inhabited part (inhabited by something other than wildlife that was) was located smack bang in the middle of the whole thing.

There had even been included, in the planning, a large number of challenges and obstacles that *weren't* part of the terrain, though there were plenty of those as well. There were even settings where whole locations could be switched around, creating almost endless possibilities when designing different races.

Harlan Illusion was as good an example of that sought after versatility needed to traverse such terrain efficiently as anyone, if you were talking horses.

The young stallion was still patiently waiting for whatever was going to happen next, though he did wish the bucket with the munchies was here; there had still been some left. Things usually got exciting when his two-legs was around and, after nearly a week cooped up amongst all the ordinariness, he thought it was about time something did.

Erina patted him affectionately, almost as if trying to ascertain that he was really there. Carefully, she reached up and adjusted the leather strap that sat around his neck. It was set with what looked like smooth grey and polished stones.

That little peculiarity had drawn more than its share of raised eyebrows since Harlan's arrival and a fair few grumblings as well.[6] There had been quite a bit of arguing over it in the yard. There had been many that didn't agree with such obvious and toy-ish displays. It was an idiotic thing to put on a horse, they thought, as if the poor creature was some sort of oversized dog. There were plenty who thought it was even down right cruel to have done so.

This was despite the large number of, sometimes, very peculiar "things" that accompanied some of the nightmares wherever they went — including

---

[6] However, his blood red, ink black, and milk white splashed paint markings hadn't. Erina often told him he looked like a joker who'd forgotten his belled cap.

one who would go into a mad rage if anyone separated them from their fluffy, pink bison plush.

However, since it was clearly stated in the horse's papers that it was not to be taken off by anyone other than his owner, grumble over it was all they did. Erina hadn't needed to ask if anyone had removed it — if they had, she was sure to have heard about it long before arriving back on the planet.

Now, while the collar might attract the odd grumble and comment, the very first thing that anyone would usually ask about, was the stallion's coat. That was to be expected. As far as Erina knew, there wasn't another one like Harlan in the whole world: *any* world.

The slim legs and delicate features of Harlan's head betrayed the desert origin of his distant ancestors. *Very* distant ancestors. There were equines in the desert at the Valley's edge, but those she'd seen didn't look anything like him.

In terms of consistency, the body still held that sleek, powerful look that suggested you were about to be bowled over by an over-friendly freight train.

But that alone didn't mark him out as any different than thousands of other horses of different kinds on Casticia's surface.

What truly made him stand out — as a horse, and not a nightmare — were his colours.

Out here, out in the sunlight, the red in Harlan's coat literally gleamed. It wasn't the red of a blood bay, though that was probably the base somewhere way down the generations, but the deep, bright red of burnished blood.

The points themselves tended towards a more conservative black, while the inky mane and tail turned white towards the ends.

What could have been mistaken for irregular stockings covered most of one leg, except it was broken up by black in places. The whole of his front knees were covered in white hairs but didn't extend either up or down.

Most of his body above this danced like a living pool of blood when he moved, though his back and rump was covered in sparse black hairs, growing thicker closer to the spine.

A thick blaze ran down the bridge of his nose, extending over the muzzle and out of all this harlequin-esque exterior looked inquisitive, bright, blue eyes.

It was as much his colours and his eyes that garnered him such attention from the less regular visitors to the yard. The rest merely shrugged and kept their opinions of such "flashy" horses to themselves. Even so, if you strained your hearing you could definitely catch the occasional snort under their breath.

Some of that might have had something to do with Seranthiem. In fact, Erina wasn't sure if it was Harlan or Sam they were keeping their distance from.

Why would they? He didn't *seem* like a bad person. A little odd, maybe. But not bad.

Erina was woken out of her contemplative reverie by a voice near her shoulder.

'Here, this will help,' Sam told her calmly, nudging her gently with a bit of ceramics.

Erina leapt up. 'Good gracious! Don't DO that!' she snapped sharply. 'Blimey. You must walk like a bloody cat … I didn't even hear you.'

Taking a few deep breaths to calm down, Erina's eyes travelled downwards to the mug he was holding. 'Ah, tea.'

'My apologies. I did not mean to startle you,' Seranthiem replied. He didn't seem to as much as twitch despite the unexpected outburst.

Nerves of steel that one, Erina thought.

'No. Right. Sorry, you just gave me such a scare,' Erina apologised awkwardly. She straightened up from where she'd been dozing against Harlan's neck with her eyes closed.

The mug was still hovering in front of her.

That must have been what had been nudging her shoulder she thought, because Sam had obviously run out of hands.

A couple of his slender fingers were looped into the ear of the brown, semi-transparent mug, while the others were holding on to a cloth bag. A saddle and blanket were draped over his right arm, the hand belonging to it holding on to the handle of a small bucket filled with bits of kit, tools, and other things. Hanging off his elbow, having slipped down from his shoulder where he'd originally put it, was a bridle.

That was why he was holding his arm so unnaturally high, she thought. He was trying to avoid the reins trailing on the ground and entangling his feet.

'Thanks,' Erina said, genuinely grateful, disentangling the mug carefully from the attached fingers.

From the mug, there arose a tantalizing aroma of sweet spring mornings and summer berries. She sniffed it appreciatively.

'This smells nice.'

'You're welcome,' Sam responded quietly.

Now, the grey bag ended up unceremoniously dumped on the ground before Sam hung the saddle and bridle on the box door. He didn't see any reason to get them dirtier than necessary — not when he was the one that had to clean them.

Rummaging around in the bag, Seranthiem brought out one of the gentler brushes and started to work on Harlan with powerful strokes. The horse wasn't dirty; he just needed a light brush down before being taken out. Also, Sam knew that it was a good time to check up on a horse, making sure that there weren't any odd bumps and scrapes that hadn't been there the last time.

'Hang on a moment, I'll give you a hand,' Erina offered.

'Please, there is no need,' Sam insisted firmly while working his way over the horse's back.

For a moment, Erina considered arguing but the journey here was taking its toll. Instead, she merely sighed and settled for sipping quietly on the strong tea which had an even sweeter flavour than its scent had suggested.

She wondered if Sam had a bit of a sweet tooth or if he'd merely tipped in the major part of the sweet-pot by accident and then made himself a more sensible cup of tea, choosing to give the first one to her rather than throwing it out.

While taking the occasional sip, blowing gently on the steaming liquid before doing so, Erina took the time to actually study the person she and her horse had seen enter their lives so unexpectedly.

Not someone who usually paid much conscious attention to what people looked like, you could have asked Erina about clothing, the approximate age, or even the species, of the last person she'd spoken to and consider yourself lucky if your answer wasn't, 'next Tuesday.'

It wasn't that she meant to be rude. It was just that things like that ... well

… slipped her mind. It didn't help that she probably hadn't been paying attention to what your question had been in the first place.

Neither of those were exactly considered positive traits in diplomatic circles; one of the many reasons she'd left the business.[7]

That didn't mean she wasn't good at seeing people for what they really were though, quite the contrary. She just wasn't aware of it most of the time. Something that annoyed her to no end was that it went as much for places as it did for people. What was the point of visiting nice new places and enjoy interesting experiences if you didn't end up remembering them properly?

'Wonder what's up with all these contemptuous looks that keep going around? Is there something I'm missing?' Erina mumbled.

She then turned those same eyes upon the one standing so casually before her. She wondered if it was any of the individual details that bothered them, or if, when they were all thrown together, they just became a little too much? It wasn't as if anyone here was poorly dressed (except those who chose it as a style), so that can't be it. Can it?

She imagined that, on many worlds, it probably was unusual to learn that the professor specializing in the atomic decay of radioactive materials was also an expert on orchids or a keen maker of ceramics. That wasn't true here, but here it also worked just as well the opposite way around; the man you depended on to look after your chickens might well be an expert on hyper engine engineering or have a side career as a famous painter.

As such, Erina knew it didn't pay to make assumptions. So that couldn't be why either.

From what she could see, he didn't seem to be using much in artificial aids in his work — albeit, she hadn't really seen him do more than play fetch so far. A lot of those working with animals preferred a more "hands-on" approach than most. Besides, so much of the technology was, by now, built in at such a fundamental level that you were hard pressed to tell it was there at all even if you did know what you were looking for.

---

[7] Though a cognitor *was* part of the diplomatic service, Erina would take offence if someone called her a diplomat. "Negotiator Extraordinaire" she could live with. Compromise was something other people did.

Just who are you? Seranthiem? Erina mulled over a thousand possible options — yet something told her that it'd be the one-thousand-and-one'th that would be the right one. The one that you would never, not even in a million years, consider.

Perhaps there was something about him that made him stand out? Could it be something really simple? Maybe it was just the way he looked? Which wasn't bad. Even she could see that.

No, bad brain. Bad, bad brain, Erina scolded it, picked up the embarrassment by the throat and threw it back in the dungeon, taking care to lock the door behind it.

She wasn't paying any attention to that. No. Not any attention at all.

As Seranthiem bent down over a back hoof, which Harlan obligingly lifted for him, he brushed a loose strand of silvery hair out of his face where it had been tickling his nose.

That long hair, which would have lent itself magnificently to being draped across his shoulders like a silver shroud, was currently being held together in a loose ponytail. At least it had probably been a ponytail once upon a time. Now, it seemed as if some of it was on a constant quest for freedom. The strands that had achieved said freedom, fluttered about in any breeze that might stop by to say hello, and tickled his nose.

Along with the delicate bones and willow-like figure, he could just as easily have stepped out of a fantastique painting and no one would have been the wiser, Erina thought. To her, he looked like he'd break if you so much as breathed at him, like a fine china cup kept to be admired rather than serving tea in (no matter how expensive the brew).

Watching him covertly, Erina wondered if he was one of those people who'd manage to look regal even when dressed in bits of an old sack tied on with a bit of rope.

'So, what brings you to these parts?' she asked off-hand.

Straightening up, Sam flicked a glance in her direction. 'I'm sorry, did you say something?'

The expression in his eyes took her back a bit. Maybe that was it, she thought as a shiver ran up her spine. His eyes alone were enough to unsettle you.

It wasn't like they were, say, the window to a soul of pure evil or something like that. It was just that, when they gazed at you, you felt as if they weren't just looking at the you today, but at the you ten years ago and the you that would be tomorrow as well as, at the same time, seeing right through you.

'What? No. I was just wondering if there's anywhere to go riding around here? Out of the way of any races or racers.'

Sam gave a small nod. 'There're continuous updates,' he said. 'If you're not yet familiar with the Court's system, let me know and I will set something up for you.'

'Good.'

'Only doing my job.'

Well, at least he isn't calling me miss or madam like everyone else, Erina sighed inwardly. Got to be grateful for something, right?

You look quite young, Erina mused to herself. But your eyes don't match the rest of you. Those pale grey globes match your appearance perfectly, they just don't fit with the image. I've seen those kinds of eyes before … somewhere … I think…

Then, trying to get to grips with her thoughts and her slowly failing eyesight, she shook her head. Why was it so hard to keep her eyelids up all of sudden?

'Why's there a red rosette on the door?' Erina wondered, tearing her attention back to the here and now. The presence of that thing had been nagging away at her consistently for some time.

Sam glanced back up again for a moment and then returned to straightening the saddle.

'That is there to ensure that everyone knows to be cautious around your horse, my lady. From the notes you provided detailing his care, I surmised that there was some sort of problem, though there were no specific details elaborating on the matter.'

A grimace came far too close to showing on her face. Erina pushed down hard. *"My lady."* It was apparently too much to ask that people didn't stick weird honorifics into a conversation with her.

Well, at least it's better than madame, she thought.

'So, there haven't been any incidences of any kind then, have there?' she asked casually.

Sam gave her a strange look. 'No, not that I'm aware of. Of course, it is possible that something might have happened and I wasn't notified.'

'Not likely,' Erina muttered quietly. If something had happened, Sam would have known about it. In fact, she felt safe betting on that nearly everyone in the vicinity would have known about it.

She resisted the urge to breathe a sigh of relief. That had been her real worry with sending Harlan here. The possibility that some poor misguided fool would go around and remove the small collar. She winced. The result would have been, how would you put it, graphic, to say the least. It hadn't been the best of times in a month for Harlan to be away from home, after all.

'No, he has been perfectly well behaved. Though I have noticed that he is not at his best if startled into awakedness early in the morning,' Sam observed.

Contrasting this with what she'd been told elsewhere, it certainly put a different perspective on things. 'There is that,' Erina admitted.

At home, that had never been a problem. Because Erina wasn't much of a morning person herself, she'd hardly ever had to deal with a grumpy Harlan. So, was it so strange that she'd completely forgotten to mention that little detail in the notes she'd prepared? She couldn't be expected to remember everything, could she?

Seranthiem adjusted the girth then swung himself up into the saddle in one smooth, effortless motion. Reins hanging loose over Harlan's neck, he bent over to adjust one of the stirrups — not that he really needed them, but they were expected.

'We will just go for a light workout around the lake at this moment. The race itself is next week, I believe.'

'Hey, I was going to go for a ride,' Erina protested loudly.

'May I suggest that some rest is in your best interest, my lady.'

Sam gave her a dismissive nod then urged the horse into a walk without a backward glance.

CHAPTER FOUR

After tossing and turning in a bed that had felt increasingly like it was determined to torture her, she finally gave up on getting any sleep, got dressed, and went out for a morning walk. A very early morning walk. She yawned her way down the winding paths leading away from her accommodations.

It was still early enough that the hazy sun-mist you got before the true start of the day was still forming. It enfolded buildings and grounds in an ethereal glowing haze, distorting shapes and erasing faults.

It was even early enough that most of the yards hadn't woken up yet either — so the only company on her little stroll were a few equally early risers among the bird population; their voices sounding somewhat subdued with the change in air density.

'Pretty songs? Yeah, if I didn't have a frigging headache already,' she grumbled.

That hot sweaty bed had done nothing for her mood. Erina sighed. Guess she'd gotten used to the more temperate climate in the Valley already. Or maybe she was simply coming down with something. Yes, that made much more sense. She put her hand to her forehead. Nope. No fever. Well, that was good.

'As if I didn't have enough to worry about,' she mumbled while paying a little less attention than she should have to where she was going.

'So, I came from there … and I was going there … so I'm? Umm? Where exactly am I?'

Sticking her hands in her pockets and rummaging around produced little result, unless you liked lint.

'Okay. Next time I go out, maybe I should actually remember to bring my diom with me? Yeah — whatever.'

Standing there, lost and still mostly asleep, she caught the sounds of shuffling along upon earthen ground.

She quietly drifted over to what turned out to be one of the open arenas. Guided more by sound than sight until a silent moon climbed to hang low in the sky, all but obscured by the clouds of rain that had drifted in during the evening before. The blue moon rose out of the mist and waters, floating high in the skies of old.

Light, blessed light of the nightday, cast eerie shadows below the mists, setting them aglow and guiding her steps.

Still half-asleep, Erina rubbed wearily at her eyes. The small noises from the arena were subdued and deadened by the floating water vapours. The sun and moon mists were intermingled, neither one thing, nor the other. It was the time when sensible people were asleep and creatures of the night were returning to their dens, while those of the day were carefully poking their noses out of their burrows, tasting the new day with tongues and eyes and noses. A time of change. Of transference. Even in today's age, it had a quality that high noon had just never been able to acquire.

When sleeping out in the forest, or even in the cabin at High Fyelds, getting up and investigating even the smallest noises outside on such a night was generally not a good idea. If, through some amazing coincidence, no trouble came of it, then you still lost sleep over it.

But what trouble could there be here, she'd wondered. While the world still held many secrets for its new inhabitants, this place had long since been settled, even landscaped. If there was anything of old hiding in the shadows in a place like this, someone was bound to have stumbled across it before, wouldn't they have?

She gulped down another breath of the moist oxygen. 'Be still, stupid nerves. There's nothing dangerous out there. And, if there is, I'll kick its ruddy ass.'

When Erina had first established High Fyelds, no, even before that, when she had first stumbled across the Valley with its lush green grass, tall forbidding mountains, and deep lakes of ice cold waters, it was obvious that it was no mere "isolated island" setting it apart from the rest of the world.

For, in the Valley, the very rules of nature as she knew them had been turned on their heads — or at the very least been seriously played around with. Harlan Illusion was very much a product of that Valley, the descendant of "normal" horses that had once lived there. And one thing that the Valley did beyond all others; it changed things, like Mordjen.

'Hah, that was an adventure, wasn't it? He scared us, sneaking around in the dark like that. What were we supposed to think? I mean, he looks like he'd gobble you up in a single bite if you got too close.'

In a way, the Valley acclimatized them to its own world, its own rules, and its own dangers — generation by generation the deep nature of the Valley growing stronger in them.

There was always a price to be paid for survival ... somewhere. And, of course, sometimes those changes came with a drawback or two. And sometimes they were downright strange. Mordjen had proven to be a friend, in the end.

But was he the exception that proved the rule? She still didn't know. And the Valley wasn't always forgiving. Far from it.

This strange place Erina had named Darklight Valley for its bright wonders and hideous nightmares that it held in equal measure, and because she didn't know its true name — if it had one. She had put aside all that had been part of her old life, and so, when the time came to once more return to the world outside, she'd taken the name of the Valley as her own.

And so, it had changed her too. It hadn't changed her penchant for lurking around in the shadows though.

She crept forwards, light on her feet, until she reached the edge of the open arena. Peering into it, she wondered what she'd see.

There should have been applause.

There should have been an audience.

There were neither.

At this hour in the morning, the indoor arena was deserted by all but a few barn swallows that had taken up residence in the rafters. Well, almost. There was what had attracted her in the first place: the low, solitary thuds of a horse in motion over soft ground.

'Fascinating,' she breathed. She'd been right. There was someone here. 'Working, even at this hour? That's some dedication.'

Erina squinted to see better.

The mist wasn't visible in here, but it still took time for her eyes to adjust to the gloom as none of the overhead lighting was actually lit, and, as such, she heard the two approach long before she could actually see them.

The 'thud' 'thud' 'thud' of the hooves on the sandy ground was the first. Then came the creaking of the harness — what little there was — and the jingle of the metal. The hot breath of the horse in the chilly air of the morning. It had all come closer and closer.

All those sounds formed a picture of their own in the mind of anyone "watching" and you were already expecting something coming — floating — towards you out of the half-shadows even before they did.

Approaching out of the gloom, a small arablike mare trotted.

It wasn't even right to call it trotting. It was more than that, far more. She moved as if she was dancing on the very edge of the air itself. Through the collected, gliding motions, you could positively "feel" the pent-up energy and power being released into every step — like a dam with all its spinners and turbines working, humming with quiet but stifled efficiency, merely hinting of what lay behind.

The majestic figure had come closer and closer.

It had been a chance thing. You know, the kind where you just happen to take a different road home and suddenly a whole new experience just opens up in front of you; one that was there all the time but which you had, none-theless, never seen before.

They'd almost seemed to move in time with the small ripples on the lake beside the arena that gently caressed the sand lining its carefully sculptured shoreline. Morning, as it was finally breaking through the sun mist, was col-ouring them blue and gold as the sun rose quietly into the sky — still veiled by a thin film of clouds set aglow by the light.

Since it was still early spring, the light "looked" warm, but once you stepped out into it, if you didn't wear enough, it had a chilly edge. Much like the sand by the lake's shore, it looked inviting at a glance but below lay a wet, moist filling that sucked at your soles.

But these two moved with an almost unnatural grace, horse and rider: Creatures of light and air and fairytales.

Erina wondered why she'd been hearing the sounds of metal clinking, as from stirrups or bit, for the horse wore neither. It wasn't wearing any saddle or bridle either for that matter. Had she'd been imagining it?

The rider seemed oblivious to this lack of tack. His arms stretched out from his body. The cloth streamed from them as they moved forward. Pale and translucent, it fluttered around itself, twisting and turning as the pinions of the wings of a bird of prey in flight.

'Sam?'

As they'd passed by, Erina saw that his eyes were closed. Yet he guided the horse with unfaltering accuracy across the arena in ever more intricate patterns until, at last, they came to a halt in the centre.

Once stationary, both hair and cloth settled down, and the long, long streamers he'd been wearing at his sleeves came to rest, much of them drifting gently to the ground.

Seranthiem looked down and noticed the gossamer like tendrils trailing beside his horse's hooves. With a few motions he began collecting them, wrapping them carefully around his arms, making sure that they didn't become entangled in the slightly shorter ones that came down from his headdress and pinned them in place.

Once he'd rolled those up as well, he fastened them securely with several of the ornamental designs that adorned the costume's head piece, shaking his sleeves loose in the process. He ran his fingers through his long hair, untangling it, and then tied it up into his customary high ponytail.

'Well done, Mirage,' Sam patted the flaxen chestnut mare. 'Very good work.'

He felt around a few pockets until his fingers met a slight bulge, then reached in and took out one of the special treats. The horse turned her head and graciously accepted what he offered her.

Then, and only then, did he turn his eyes towards their watcher.

'Spying on others would seem beneath you, my lady. It is quite unbecoming,' he said coldly.

Wanting nothing less than to shout at him that he couldn't be more wrong, Erina's teeth had clenched,

And with that, Seranthiem had turned his horse with a gentle touch. And without leads, the arabesque mare following him like an adoring puppy, he'd walked off, out of the arena.

'Coldblooded, bloody jerk!' Erina fumed.

Further along in the morning, when the rest of the world had woken up as well, Erina hadn't been too keen on going down to the horses and encountering him again. Not sure if she could resist doing something likely to get her in trouble — like breaking a leg or two. She hated being told off — even more so when she felt there really wasn't any call for it.

It wasn't like she'd pretended to hide or anything. If she had, he wouldn't have noticed her. She was sure of that. Hiding was one of her specialities. It was far easier to find things out that way — not to mention a surprise attack gave you all sorts of advantages. It had been a highly useful skill in her old job.

She'd just been curious as to what was going on. There had been no reason to accuse her of doing something as crude as spying. The arena wasn't exactly a secret hideout or something, now was it? And it wasn't as if he'd bothered to stick a notice on the door: something saying, "training, don't disturb."

She continued muttering darkly to herself all morning, approaching the noon hour in a foul mood.

As such, it was more than odd, the next time she saw Seranthiem, that he acted like if it had never happened at all.

'Well, if you want to pretend, then so can I, stupid.'

A full day later, once Erina managed to control the urge to have her teeth introduce themselves to Sam's jugular, they were standing outside Harlan's stall.

'So, what's that for?' Erina asked.

'Hmm, which what?' Seranthiem pulled his eyes from the bridle in his hands.

'That.' Erina pointed to what he was holding.

It wasn't that she didn't know what a bridle was — though all she used at home was a bit of shaped rope — but that hadn't been the question.

'That!' Erina made another stabbing motion. 'What you're doing.'

'Maintenance,' Sam said, as if that explained everything.

Erina rolled her eyes at him, so he continued, 'your horse chews on his bit so the leather grows stiff. This is rach hide, so while not liable to break, this helps soften it. Makes it more comfortable.'

'I'm not surprised. I've never used a bit.'

It had been several days since arriving, and they all seemed to begin much the same. It wasn't as if she was trying to be annoying on purpose, but that sure seemed to be the way Seranthiem was thinking of her.

So, she didn't know the names of every bit of scrap leather, the one-thousand-and-one uses for clasps and straps, or even the best way to saddle up a horse. An annoying, inexperienced dimwit from the far, far away, that's what it made her feel like.

Well, was it her fault that the Valley didn't use *any* of that stuff? It was an untamed place where the inhabitants were no less wild than the nature. Visiting wasn't like taking a stroll in the park with umbrellas and maybe the promise of a picnic.

Erina looked up, shielding her eyes from the sun. It was the beginning of a nice day by the looks of it. At least, the weather was cooperating then.

A nice day such as this — actually, any day at all when you thought about it — when you could see a yellow disc hanging in the sky like a golden jewel; a loving sun caressing the land with its gentle yellow light and some white cotton bud clouds drifting lazily across the sky. It was almost impossible to imagine that that was only what it looked like from down here.

In a way it was kind of odd, the way there was only one sun in the heavens when you gazed skywards, Erina thought. *Very* odd, even. And, following that, you'd have expected, once you reached beyond the atmosphere, to find, hanging there in space, a giant ball of gas burning itself as it went.

But that wasn't what was out there. Or, more accurately, that wasn't the *only* thing that was out there. She hadn't really believed it at first despite reading and learning about it — not completely truly believed it — until she'd seen it with her own eyes. No one did. It defied every ounce of common sense.

'Tell me, Sam. Have you ever been off planet?'

'I'm quite occupied here.'

'I'm better with ships. They make more sense. They either work or they don't.'

'I believe a ship's engineer or mechanic might dispute this, my lady,' Sam almost chuckled. Somehow, he couldn't see this small human being in space.

'It makes you feel, well, free,' Erina said. 'The Valley, it has the same feeling. There's just something "more" to it. Like a weight's been lifted from your shoulders and when you open your eyes you can see far, so far. You get a lot of the unexpected there.'

Unexpected was the word when it came to the sun, too. For once you had left the atmosphere and gotten out into space proper that single yellow star that you could see and measure from the ground was merely one of many. Many, many even.

Once you got into space, there they hung. Like a gaudy necklace of shining pearls in all shapes and sizes, six stellar objects of varying proportions and colours danced their intricate dance in the centre of the solar system.

The further you got from the planet, the stronger the gravitational pull of those stars became too.[8]

They could be seen clearly with your own eyes but, so far, they defied every single attempt at measuring it — to say nothing about every explanation that they'd come up with.

According to the scientists this was impossible, riding in opposite of every known law of physics and science, and a fair few that were only suspected.

The stars didn't know that.

The stars didn't care.

It didn't stop it from being true. And Darklight Valley was just as impossible. Filled with just as much mystery.

There were theories, of course, about the stars. Simple theories. Complicated theories. Wild theories. Even just plain old boring theories, for "why"

---

[8] Which made perfect sense. Until you realized that the force should have torn the planet you just left apart. Casticia was a planet where no planet had the right to be. It didn't care and was there anyway.

it was like that. The only thing they all had in common was that none of them actually worked.

Indeed, the ships moving around the solar system either timed their journeys to make sure they didn't get caught outside, and pulled in, or took quite the detour to avoid the same fate. Subsequently, they normally never strayed into the area between their home planet's orbit and the suns … except by accident. Very fatal accidents, usually.

Erina shrugged. It wasn't her problem at the moment. There were plenty of unexplained things down here on the surface without trying to wrap your head around those in space as well. And though she couldn't explain why, she had a feeling they were somehow connected.

Oh well … best to leave herself some work for tomorrow then.

'Does this mean once you're done with that, I can finally go riding?'

'If you wish. Most owners preparing for the Stakes keep to quite a strict regime of training.'

'If I didn't know better, I'd believe you were accusing me of gallivanting around. Harlan's a *horse*, not some toy waiting to be primped and spoiled.'

Not that Harlan didn't get spoilt, or Mordjen either for that matter — just not "that" way.

'Very well. I will make the necessary preparations.'

'Good. You do that.'

🐎 🐎 🐎

Shortly after, the sounds of yet another pair of hooves made Erina tear herself away from watching where a grey gelding was getting liberal amounts of water splashed about while being sponged down.

Sam was leading two horses, both tacked up with a minimal amount of gear.

One of them was her own, Harlan Illusion, looking his usual handsome self. He was prancing about excitedly at the end of a lead. Ears pricking forward at the sight of her and he whinnied happily. He was a bit bored with taking sedate runs on the lawn, but now, with his own two-legs here, slow and steady wasn't going to be the order of the day.

'Who's that?' Erina nodded at the newest arrival, a well-muscled buckskin with four, irregular socks and a bald face.

'This is Wave Rock,' Sam threw the reins over the horse's head. 'He is my partner here.'

He swung himself up with fluid grace. 'I believe we will depart sooner if you were to actually mount your horse, my lady.'

Growling something rude under her breath, Erina clicked her tongue and placed one foot in the stirrup as Harlan trotted up. Whatever today was going to be, it was already getting on her nerves. Now she couldn't even have a nice, lonesome ride all to herself.

'Are you coming?' Sam asked from the already moving Wave Rock.

'Drat. Yeah, sure.' Erina collected the reins in one hand as she struggled to get her gloves on and nudged Harlan forwards.

The excited trias didn't need much encouragement and gladly danced after the other pair.

They trotted across their own yard, hooves clip clopping on the hard surface, passed between a couple of barren walls, and, after a few turns, reached the open lands beyond the gate.

It felt good to be back in the saddle, though she still wasn't used to actually using one. In and out between small copses of trees, on trails well maintained yet rugged, they rode. Erina was soon gritting her teeth at the slow pace Seranthiem was setting. It was great if you were a pack-mule, less so if you enjoyed to stretch your legs to the full.

They'd almost completed their first circuit when commotion appeared before them.

'Come on!' the voice ahead strained against the weight of the reins. 'It's just a stupid sheet! Move!'

The grey gelding, ears flattened against his skull, just dug his hooves in even further into the soft dirt. He wasn't going anywhere near that flapping great thing. And he wasn't going past it either thank you very much — carrots or no carrots.

'Sorry, mam,' one of the handlers bumped into her as he moved past and apologised before hurrying off to remove the offending object.

The sheet was flapping quite happily in the wind, caught on a couple of low branches of hawthorn and completely unaware of all the commotion it was causing.

It was snatched up and shredded by a passing, charcoal-coloured slime-ball on four legs before its handlers were able to drag it away. The other horses shied away from the passing nightmare, whose large, yellow eyes flittered coldly from scene to scene, scanning for weaknesses.

As the men pulled it out of sight, the other horses relaxed noticeably, along with their riders. And after several snorts, the gelding walked on.

'Don't believe they'll have much luck with that one until they get a few things sorted, I think,' someone passing by grunted disgustedly.

'Certainly a different set of priorities,' Seranthiem agreed calmly.

Sam was leaning on the fence to one of the paddocks, watching some of the airs-above-ground practice.

'I saw him run the other day. He seems a friendly horse, just not a very confident one,' Erina said.

'Not like Wave Rock. Not like Mirage.' Erina nodded sagely. She'd met Mirage earlier one morning and the whole thing still felt a bit unreal. 'What is it with you and horses? Rock's about as unflappable as a tank.'

'True,' Sam replied mildly. I do not believe that you could say that he is. I wouldn't have put it quite like that, though.'

Erina leaned on the semblance-wood fence. She was still annoyed with him, but, so far, he seemed as unflappable as the horses he cared for. So turning that annoyance into action was pointless.

She sighed. 'It'd be so much easier if I could punch you.'

'Sorry, did you say something?'

'What? No... nothing. Nothing at all.'

Erina sighed again. All this so-called "social-interaction" was exhausting — and supposedly she wasn't even good at it. It didn't help that she was still tired, still not having gotten much sleep.

Now, standing here so casually, watching someone else's' practice, things were, mostly, back to normal.

'Maybe there's a human being in there somewhere, after all.'

Well, maybe not quite. Erina still caught the feeling that she was somehow trespassing on his personal space and he'd get everything done much, much quicker if she wasn't around. But it wasn't quite as pronounced as when they'd first met.

'That one,' Sam, choosing not to understand most of Erina's random mutterings, nodded towards a pale chestnut that was being put through their paces not ten yards away, 'doesn't let it affect her at all,' he observed knowingly. 'Outside stimulus does not bother her. On the other hand, and for very much the same reason, she needs more work on paying attention to the cues from her rider. But she is young and has come a long way already with her trainer since he got her.'

Erina took a second look. But no matter how hard she tried, she couldn't notice anything like that at all.

'How can you tell,' she asked curiously.

Seranthiem treated her to a small, but ultimately secretive, smile.

'I just do.'

CHAPTER FIVE

Ahead, usually so gentle and having rested comfortably on the white fence only a moment earlier, suddenly snaked forward. Harlan's teeth snapped around the loose end of the scarf and tossed it up into the air.

'Nooo... Harlan... Bad horse!'

Erina made a grab for the long, white piece of cloth. Her fingers clutched at empty space.

The stallion threw his head from side to side while running around the yard, rearing and bucking to his heart's content, the scarf tossed about by breeze and horse alike.

It wasn't the first time.

Erina chased after him. 'Get back here you little pest!'

Harlan neighed and easily danced out of the way as she grasped for the scarf. It was so simple to keep it out of reach, keeping just one step away. He snorted, backing up against the sycamore trees.

Ears pointed firmly forward, eyes glued to his person. If horses could grin, he would have been grinning. He hadn't had this much fun in quite some time.

'Harlan. Be a good horsie and give that back. There's a good boy,' Erina pleaded with him.

The trias snorted again. His eyes glittered like dark tide pools on a spring morning — so full of promise and mischief. Harlan scratched the ground with his right hoof. While he couldn't understand some things that his human said, he knew that tone of voice well enough, but this was far too much fun to just give up on.

Erina sighed and went after him again. It seemed like it was going to be that kind of day...

Two hours later and it still hadn't improved much. If anything, it was slowly climbing the epic scale of awfulness, which began at a splinter in your foot and ended with having your body dismembered by a black hole. Hopefully it'd stop before it got carried away. Hopefully.

'Cough ... splutter ... cough...'

The sounds of someone squelching their way to shore drifted in on the wind.

'Gross!' Erina spit out a bit of lake water mingled with horse hair and some sort of algae.

She shivered. The water was less than pleasant, even if you *didn't* count what was growing in it. She was sure she'd felt something wiggling about her toes — and she was wearing boots.

Even after a full day in the sun — the lake hiding in the shadows of wide oaks and slender birch — the water might have looked warm and inviting. 'Yeah, if you're a mermaid maybe,' Erina spit out some more water. 'Urgh. Gack. Eew.'

Her hair, plastered against her head and face, was already soaked from when she'd gone under after falling off, as was the rest of her, even if now, when sitting up, the water only reached just above her chest.

She picked some more of the green gunk out of her hair and, after a few false tries on the slippery bottom, managed to get to her feet and struggled ashore.

'Great impression we're making today, Harlie,' she chided the horse, who was patiently waiting in the shallows for her to catch up, trying out the taste of the local reeds.

'First you decide to play tag with my clothes and then you dunk me in the nearest bit of water you're able to find.' Erina patted his muzzle distractedly. 'You're quite the troublemaker today, aren't you? Are you sure you're not part kelpie or something?'

She sighed morosely at the thought of going back like this. 'Drenched. Drowned like the proverbial rat. If they didn't laugh their sides off about us already, they're sure to do so now.'

Erina gathered up the loose reins and coaxed Harlan out of the water. After a few hops, she swung her leg over and back up into the saddle. She landed with a resolute squelch and winced.

Nudging the horse forwards, Erina reached up to rub off some of the water on her face with her sleeve. Instead of getting cleaner, it just managed to smear the mud over the remaining bits of face that had, somehow, managed to avoid being dragged into the water/mud/skin confrontation.

'Oh well. Guess we should just head back. I think we've made enough of an idiot of ourselves for one day, wouldn't you say?'

She clicked her tongue and Harlan obediently broke into a trot. 'I mean, I know I named you after a kind of joker, but couldn't you be a little less, you know... *you*!'

Harlan flicked an ear in her direction while she was talking, but if he was having any second thoughts, he sure was keeping them to himself.

That little swim was why, an hour or so later, it was with a particularly contented sigh that Erina turned off the hot water streaming from the showerhead above.

She reached out for the towels she'd placed conveniently close before getting in — no reason to step out and slip on some wet patches if it could be helped — and draped one around her hair, having first wrung it out, then the other around her body. It wasn't exactly a toga but that was what it reminded her of every time she stepped out of the shower.

'I really should stop thinking like that. It's becoming a bit too much like an old habit,' she muttered. 'We all know old habits can get you killed.'

'Things sure have changed since I got involved with this horsey business.' They had changed a lot. Erina wondered if *she* had been changing as well. Casting a passing glance at her reflection in the mirror, she grimaced and turned away. Some things *never* changed.

It had been nice indeed getting all those traces of green "stuff" out of her hair — though a good super-heated shower didn't need a reason to be appreciated. It generally made you feel fresh and ready to face the world anew. It worked wonders on sore muscles too. It was getting a bit close in here though.

'Maybe I ought to let in some air?' Erina looked around her. Most of the bathroom was wrapped in a slight haze, steam from the heated water still hung in the air. Tugging at the towel that was already making its bid for freedom and wrapping it tighter and more securely than before, she stepped over to the window, unlocked it, and pushed it open, ever so slightly.

'There, that's better,' she said. 'Now, to find something to wear then?' Erina almost growled. 'Great, more decisions.'

She frowned again. 'What a mess. Since when did I practice floor/bed filing?' She shook her head and started to pick up things. 'Oh, hello — haven't seen you since I packed,' Erina threw the tiny box on the bedside table.

As she did so, she noticed something white and square sticking out from underneath a worn, black shirt. 'Well, what do we have here?'

Picking it up and turning it over, her eyes glanced over it casually, checking to see it if it was anything important. It was a meeting request. It was also for five minutes ago, today.

'Whoops,' Erina's mind caught up with her eyes and poked her sharply in the guilt region.

That was the downside of rarely being reachable by diom these days. Those that knew her had to resort to more old-fashioned contact methods. The type that didn't come with an alarm.

'Hold on just a second, this could actually be interesting,' she hummed to herself as she put the note down again and began to dress at a speed a small hurricane would have been proud of. 'It's been a while after all.'

Strapping on a slim blade and pulling her trouser-leg down to cover it she finished up by tying back her unruly hair and shoving a small blaster into a holster under her jacket.

And so, trusting those assigned to her to keep preparing for the competition without her breathing down their necks, Erina picked up her coat and stepped out.

It wasn't difficult making her way into the city, once she'd ducked to avoid a particularly nasty grey slime-ball who'd decided he hadn't been fed enough today — or maybe he'd just wanted dessert. What did she know? She'd stepped on-board the local transport as the trainers tried to haul the sinuous nightmare away.

There wasn't actually much in terms of traffic and the transporter managed to drop her off just outside the address she'd been given. She thought that was unusually convenient, knowing her usual luck with that sort of thing.

That had been half an hour ago. Right now, Erina regarded the piece of cake sitting before her suspiciously. It was a *suspicious* cake. For all it was a beautiful creation; all spun sugar and whipped cream draped across it like a bridal veil, it looked like it was up to something, she thought.

The cake remained silent on the matter.

Her companion watched her stoically, having long ago gotten used to the silences that so often surrounded his former Cognitor. Not being a great believer in talking when she had nothing important to say — around people that was — there were a lot of those.

Sometimes he found it slightly unnerving. Along with the look in her eyes that alternated between "yes, I know everything you're hiding and isn't there something you want to give me?" and "your existence in this universe is bothering me, go away!" It was a great trait in her former profession, but it did make you watch your back.

It wasn't the best of traits when working in enclosed spaces together with others though, not for prolonged periods of time, he had to admit that. There hadn't been many with a pass to the bridge that could make everyone tense up for long after they'd actually left. Still, she'd always been good at her job, he reminded himself. Remarkably so, considering her age when he'd hired her.

'How's this new life of yours treating you then?' Tom Treee asked cautiously.

'It's different, I suppose,' she conceded.

The man on the opposite side of the small table just took another bite of the gateau he'd ordered with his hot drink, adjusting his thoughts to the general mood as he did so.

'Sleeping under the stars. Roaming the wild forests with the beasts of the land and the birds of the sky and generally roughing it? A bit different, yeah,' he agreed as a somewhat coarse laughter escaped his throat.

It earned him a short, sharp scowl in his general direction. '*Thank you* for your concise and accurate summary of the situation!' Erina snapped pointedly.

Ouch, Treee thought. Bit of a sensitive spot there. Best to avoid that one then. He coughed delicately.

'So, it's treating you ok then?' he asked again, honest concern radiating from his words.

Even with his large, robust appearance looking decidedly out of place among the delicate china of the small tea shop, he still managed to look worried.

Treee continued as he received no answer. 'I hear the racing circuit can be pretty harsh. Can't say for sure though, never raced anything myself.'

Erina chortled. 'Only because the competitors would have taken one look at you and run away.'

'I always figured it was 'cause I couldn't fit into the cockpit of one of those miniships,' he grinned disarmingly.

Pretending to lean back and give him a once over with her eyes, 'Can't imagine why,' she quipped. 'Maybe if we divided you in half, you'd be enough for two normal people.'

'But not twice as good a Captain!'

'True.'

Erina was grateful that they were sitting down. Standing next to him she always felt *extra* small and, being a somewhat slightly built female in the first place, she didn't need any help with that.

For if Tom Treee was imposing enough when sitting down, on his feet, he towered above her. Actually, at practically two meters in height without his boots on, Tom Treee towered over most of the crew. On the merely physical side, he appeared to be able to squash her like a bug and with about as much effort.

As she'd pointed out, his huge barrel like chest and arms rippling with muscles underneath the neat shirt and jacket made a good attempt at taking up the space of the average bear. Since the rest of him followed along the same lines, you'd have expected him to have used brute strength to break up arguments or barrelling into a plasma field.

He didn't. Erina wondered if that's why they'd worked so well together.

Two people, neither quite what they seemed, and perfectly happy to play off that to throw people off their guards. She had to admit, it *had* been handy.

She'd always thought it was useful for seeing things others couldn't in a crowd and it was great knowing someone like that had your back. Also very handy to have around when you couldn't get those stubborn nutrilicious jars to open.

Tom, on the other hand, always said it was mostly a nuisance trying to fit into spaces clearly not designed with those like him in mind. At which point, Erina would usually remind him that she had exactly the same problem, only the other way around. Did he have any idea what a pain trying to drive or fly something was when you couldn't even reach the controls?

Whatever had persuaded him to go into space, with — despite being, essentially, one big space — its customary small, tight and often crammed areas between walls that kept the bit of space where you could breathe from the bit of space where you could, well, not — was beyond her understanding.

Not that all ships were like that.

There could be no doubt that he belonged out there though. He was, when all was said and done, more than just good at what he did. He was one of the best.

Treee had been the Captain of the *Random Star* when she'd first joined. He hadn't been all that keen on the idea of her joining the crew back then as she recalled. Still, he'd been willing to give her a chance — and that was more than others had done. For that, she would always be grateful. If he needed a hand with something, she'd have his back. Somehow, she didn't think he'd invited her because he suddenly wanted a horse.

Erina had to keep herself from laughing out loud. The image of the Captain on a horse was nothing short of hilarious. Suppose, if we dressed him up, he'd be good to play Barbarian Exhibit A, she chuckled.

'You know. I'd never have figured you for the going back to basics type Erina,' Treee said.

'Running a stable is hardly "back to nature" you know,' Erina countered flatly. 'I have one horse. One! Okay, one and a half if you count Mordjen when he drops by.'

'Come on. You used to volunteer for patrol duty just so that you wouldn't have to go on shore leave. You *never* volunteer for anything.'

'Are you referring to my tactical decision to refuse to be pulled into the customary bar fight and drinking games that always followed? Your point being?' Erina retorted coldly.

'You and grass just don't match up in my mind. That's what I'm saying. That's all.' Tom took a large gulp of his favourite beverage.

'Grass is fine. It's people I could do without.'

'Still avoiding them?' Tom wondered.

'Sure I am. The Valley isn't exactly prime property for a holiday resort you know,' Erina scoffed.

'I meant *here!*' Tom gave her a stern look, waving his hand around.

'I know what you meant. I'm just saying, that's all. Mostly I get the place to myself. The animals don't count, not even the ones whose type of greeting involves trying to *eat* me,' Erina insisted.

'It is safe, isn't it?'

'Define safe?' Erina shrugged. 'No, actually … don't.'

'You're not going to get yourself squashed by one of these new "discoveries" of yours, are you?'

'It's not on my to-do list, no,' Erina grinned.

Treee gave up. 'I'm your Commanding Officer. I'm sure you're not supposed to argue with me,' he said.

'*Were!*'

'Didn't stop you back then. Most pig-headed crewmember I've ever had, including me.'

Erina stuck her tongue out at him.

Yup, still the same old Erina. Tom offered a wry grin. He'd never won an argument with her — not actually, properly "won" — in all the time they'd worked together. He didn't know anyone else who had either. Even if you got the last word in, she still gave the impression that you'd just put down, proudly, a perfect hand in a card game only to find that your opponent had been playing shogi all along.

She was the type to bring a blade to a gunfight and, afterwards, you didn't quite understand why she was the only one standing.

Sometimes you didn't discover this until later. Very, very much later.

Erina might have the patience of a hyped squirrel when it came to people (and machines) but had the endurance of a sage when it came to waiting until the pendulum once again swung in your favour and the bells of Karma called you home. It was like trying to win an argument with a small, friendly black hole. Whatever else might happen, it was still a gravitational singularity.

But then, she was the kind of person who could turn 'good morning' into the century's greatest insult if she felt like it.

'You always were contradictory,' Tom said. Now that he thought about it "contradictory" was probably the most describing word in the entire dictionary for her. "Chameleon" was a good second though.

Sometimes he wondered how she ever managed to make any decisions at all. Every second, countless scenarios and possibilities and outcomes based on everything from fact and figures to gut feelings seemed to run through her mind — not that she seemed to have to actively think about them — it was more like some great analytical computer was running somewhere in the background, and she just picked and chose what was important enough to pay attention to. Of course, when the hiccups happened — and they did — things could go from dull to "oh my god, we're going to die" very fast.

'Efficient though,' Erina countered after a speck of silence.

'True,' Tom rubbed his chin. Personally, he suspected that "at heart" she would rather knock someone over the head with a bit of steel piping than develop a constructive argument. Maybe it was because it took her so much effort not to do so, that she was such a skilled negotiator?

Either that or she was just naturally inclined to wriggle her way out of things — especially through giving others the impression that it had been their idea from the start. What was it she'd said once? "A fool follows unquestioningly. A wise man guides. A *sensible* person makes sure that things go their way without anyone ever knowing."

'You're really going to toughen this out then? It won't be easy you know.'

'I know,' Erina agreed pleasantly, taking a sip from the, by now, lukewarm tea.

'Well, if you need anything, anything at all, just give a holler. I'm sure to give you a good estimate of time,' Treee offered.

'Thanks,' she muttered mutinously. 'I'll be sure to remember that the next time I'm in the market for interplanetary "transport."'

The Captain continued as if he hadn't heard her. 'I'm sure we can squeeze it in somewhere.' His lips twitched before finally erupting into an amiable, raucous laugh.

'Incidentally,' he leaned forwards, lowering his voice. 'You haven't seen any evidence of you-know-what in that valley of yours, have you?'

'Am I supposed to know what you're talking about?'

'You know … *dragons*. You've seem 'em, *real* ones I mean? Not these new-fangled ones. I mean *really* real ones. All fire and brimstone and protecting their hoard and all that.' He looked at her eagerly.

'What? Fairytale Dragons? No, I haven't seen anything like that up at High Fyelds.'

Tom sagged a bit, looking disappointed.

'Of course, I haven't had much chance of exploring — there's a lot of terrain up there you know.'

'Yes, yes … of course. It's just … I'd really like to know what the "old" ones were like. I mean, even if you find some bones or even footprints, that'd be great,' Treee pleaded, straightening up again.

'I'll try to remember,' Erina promised, trying not to chuckle out loud. 'By the way, what did you mean by "new-fangled" ones? Have they made even more of them?'

'Well, Erina, my dear. You *have* been a bit out of touch, haven't you?'

'No need to go rub it in,' her mouth developed a thin line mirroring her eyes and causing Tom to wave his hands in front of him disarmingly.

'Now, now, there's no need for that.'

'Come on, can't you just tell me instead of stalking around the subject like a kitten around a ball of yarn?'

'Oh well, if you're gonna be like that.' Treee settled back. 'I don't know all that much about it myself really — not more than what's official anyway. But the story goes that some explorers, cave enthusiasts really, stumbled across some weird looking bits of rock years and years ago. Only, when they took them back home, they turned out not to be rocks at all but fossilized bits of horn and bones and eggs.'

'Tom. That I know. We *all* know. We've all seen them. I still don't get how they got from that to actual, living, breathing dragons. Some bits of ancient bones don't make a dragon. In fact, it's about as far from making a dragon as you can get — on account of the bones being, well … dead.'

Erina shook her head obstinately and stirred some more sweetener into her reheated tea, having given up the cake as a bad job after the first bite. Looked great. Tasted revolting.

'If you didn't interrupt, I might get to that point,' Tom suggested bluntly.

'Only if you're not so longwinded. I like my explanations short and concise.'

'Anyway—' Tom continued stoically. 'Some scientist somewhere studied them for decades and decades — you know that there's hardly any evidence for what this world was like back in the old days. Anyway, apparently someone decided to start experimenting on them. Some myth-loving crackpot decided to try and bring them back and that's what started it. Supposedly.'

'Great big lizards that fly and breathe fire? Oh yeah, I can see how that was a good idea,' Erina snorted sarcastically. 'So, why haven't we've been hearing about random ransacked villages and maidens chained to bits of rock then?'

'You've got to not confuse the myths with reality. Or,' and here Tom hesitated, 'at least with what we know as reality. That's why I'd really like to know more about what dragons used to be around here. *Our* dragons aren't anything like that.'

'There's a big research station out towards Hollow Mountains. That's where they are. Haven't seen one up close though. There's even a rumour going around that some of them … they can change shape.'

'Chameleon dragons?' Erina rolled her eyes at him. 'You've been reading too many stories. 'Okay, okay, I promise to look real careful at the dustbins from now on in case one of them's a dragon in disguise.'

'You're being difficult again.'

'I suppose,' Erina massaged her temples with her forefingers.

'Stressed?'

'A little,' Erina admitted sheepishly. 'Too bad you can't do these kinds of things long distance.'

Tom took "these kinds of things" to mean racing, not the current conversation. He thought it was safer that way.

'You should eat your cake. You look like you could do with the sugar. You're gonna disappear one of these days.' He pushed the plate towards her.

'Sure, sure. I'll remember that. But not that one!' Erina gathered her things together, preparing to leave. 'Disgusting thing. You can have it if you'd like. In the meantime, I'll look into this for you,' Erina tapped the info he'd transferred to her diom. 'I should have something for you shortly. Might take a bit longer than usual — I'm going to be pretty busy these next few days.'

'So, when's the big date?'

'Tomorrow,' Erina answered promptly. 'You'll watch, won't you?'

'Wouldn't miss it,' Tom assured her. 'Hang in there, kiddo.' He gave her a thumbs up as they parted company outside the café.

CHAPTER SIX

It seemed time flashed past at lightspeed, for, before she knew it, tomorrow was upon them.

Harlan snorted, bending down and snapping at the black cloth they were insisting on wrapping around his legs.

'There now, boy, none of that please,' Erina shifted her balance where she squatted by the horse's front legs.

Harlan buffed her again and tried to munch on her jacket instead.

'And none of that either,' she chided him. 'Behave, or I'll tie the lead rope to the other side of the walkway too.'

'No need to fret my friend. You will be fine,' Seranthiem continued with his brushing, using the same long, sweeping strokes as usual.

Not that there was all that much left to brush. Harlan's bright colours were already gleaming, his coat spotless.

An agitated sound from one of the other boarders made Sam look over his shoulder. 'And you can be quiet as well! I am certain that none of us are impressed.'

'Ignore them Harlie, they're just jealous,' Erina crooned soothingly as the stallion twitched. He'd never been comfortable with aggressors at home. Didn't look like there was much difference when he was away, she thought.

'I do not believe that these bandages agree with him,' Sam commented, raising a small cloud of dust and hair when cleaning out the brush.

'Of course they don't. He's a proper *working* horse! Not one of these pampered lapdogs,' Erina scoffed at the very thought. 'But they're regulation issue for today. They can be annoying like that here.' She sighed morosely.

'You are merely displeased because you can not take part yourself, my lady.' Sam tried to avoid that small, knowing smile but it was hard.

'Stupid rule!' Erina muttered darkly. 'How was I supposed to know you had to be registered as an officially available rider with the association weeks ahead?' Aside from that it probably had said so in the paperwork … somewhere.

It was a good thing that Sam couldn't see her face, crouched down as she was. Thunderclouds might have been more impressive but not even they could hold the same cold menace that, for but a moment, flittered across Erina's features.

Then, straightening up and brushing off her hands on her trousers, she tossed the remaining bandages back into the box, as if nothing had happened.

'Anyway—'

'Yes?'

'You two better make a good showing of yourself today. I know it's our first big race, but that doesn't make it any less important. There're a lot of specialized *and* general stables taking part. It's a good chance to see and be seen, if you know what I mean. And it's important that they see the right things, not the wrong ones.'

Sam took Erina's lecturing in stride. She wasn't telling him anything he didn't already know.

The normal invitations for the Phoenix Stakes were sent out weeks, if not months, in advance, so that there'd be plenty of time to prepare. But for the "open" slots you could get a notice a day before the actual run.

'I think—'

'You're right. I suppose I should count myself lucky I had any advance warning at all. It's not like this place is a hop, skip and jump from High Fyelds.'

'I do not believe I'm familiar with this location?'

'Hah! I bet you aren't. No one else is.' Erina rubbed at her temples. 'It's going to get quite inconvenient … eventually. Gets full points for privacy though,' she chuckled.

Looking out over the nearby stables, Erina winced. The "track" for today was in excellent condition, but the scattered rain they'd had during the early morning made her glad she'd not need to run it herself. It smelled damp and fresh. A glistening film covered everything and every little ray of sunshine seemed to bounce around several times from their reflections. The rustling of wet leaves could be heard as both the wind and the birds were once again coming out of hiding.

There was growing, kind of hectic chaos around them. The type where everything happens against all common sense saying they should have, in fact, turned into a miscellaneous equine soup — with some human garnishes on the side.

Some thrived under such conditions. Erina wasn't one of them. And judging from his fidgeting, neither was Harlan.

She patted him comfortingly on the shoulder. 'You promise you'll look after him?'

'Of course,' Sam assured her.

For Harlan, this was going to be his first proper race. For High Fyelds, it was the first time anyone would see them. They'd be playing for keeps. It was the only way.

By the time the main event of the day was getting ready to start, the handsome, quiet trias looked about. His head was held high. His movement's graceful, if a bit jittery.

'Easy,' Sam stroked his neck just below the mane. 'There's nothing to be concerned of.'

Many of the other participants would have disagreed with him, had they heard him over the din. Everywhere you looked, there were equines and humans.

In between the snorts and neighs of the horses came the challenging cries of a nightmare. The more sedate ones mingled within the throng of bodies moving about, always moving about. It was as if none, today, were capable of standing still.

At the outskirts of the undulating mass of bodies, factors struggled with those nightmares that refused to settle.

Their eyes gleamed. They weren't interested in the race. They didn't care for the humans trying to stay on their backs. All they saw was prey. They couldn't wait to give chase. To play with them. To catch up, ripping into the flanks with their fangs. Slicing them with their talons.

'Don't worry. No one is going to eat you,' Sam pushed Harlan through the milling crowd of stomping, snorting equines.

Harlan had drawn a fair few eyes already, just standing there. Now he became lost, just another warm body amongst so many others. The Phoenix Stakes always drew a large crowd: racers and viewers alike.

There were owners, trainers, riders, pets, and couples and families just out for the day. There were even crews on shore-leave looking for a quick score. Everything and everyone was turning up — and if they couldn't be there in person, they tuned in.

And that wasn't even counting a whole miniature army of information brokers working their different angles; their small mobile broadcasters hovering faithfully over their heads.

Not everyone agreed with the inclusion of nightmares or anything else that didn't conform to their idea of what a horse should be.

'What a joke,' someone spat spitefully.

'Add a bit of green and he could pass for a leprechaun. He's about the right size,' another quipped disdainfully as Harlan passed by.

'Nah, leprechauns don't have four legs,' a third grunted unpleasantly.

'How d'you know? Have you ever seen one?' the first man raised an eyebrow at his companion.

'Dude! It was a joke. There's no such thing as a leprechaun,' the other rolled his eyes.

It was a good thing Erina couldn't hear them where she stood. She didn't need any further reason to be nervous … or angry. Her right hand clenched tightly again and again, as she tried to calm down.

'Don't listen to them buddy. They have no idea!' Erina whispered to her horse from afar.

Harlan Illusion shook his head, mussing up his carefully brushed mane, and stepped forward daintily. Seranthiem tightened his grip on the reins, just in case.

He knew that, while small and slightly built, the seemingly fragile frame of the tricoloured horse belied his endurance. But that wouldn't do any of them any good if he got injured before the race had even started. And from the angry screams up ahead *someone* was having a very bad day.

From where he was sitting, Sam could feel the stirring growing. That queasy feeling that grows when your body hears things that your ears cannot.

Ahzzadel's Tzar wasn't much bigger than Harlan, but he tore into the ground, kicking and screaming as he tried to get at a much larger black horse.

'Woah! Woah!' his rider called out, clinging on for dear life.

The slithery grey mount pulled his handlers around, lashing out with hooves at the other horses, yellow snake eyes shining with malice. Snapping shut his fanged jaws just inches away from the black's neck, his rider pulled his head away with only moments to spare.

A winner he might be, if for no other reason than none of the competition wanting to get close to him. But he had a bad habit of putting his teeth into the other runners, humans and horses alike, if he got half the chance.

Sam shuddered. There was an equine he was glad he'd never been asked to work with. Ahzzadel's very presence made him feel like being coated in gunge and then fed something even grosser.

Beneath him, Harlan turned to snuffle at the saddle that had been laid across his back as Sam bent over to check the girth. This place wasn't any-where to fall off. Out there, in the actual race, it wouldn't be the best thing to happen to him either.

His "family" was nice enough but even so. This place was a bit too noisy for his liking and too crowded by far. Harlan's nostrils flared. Oh, and on top of that some of the residents here seemed less than friendly themselves.

Harlan ignored the angry screams coming from one of the strange crea-tures further down as Ahzzadel was pulled away by force. That one had arrived a while back. So far he'd already kicked five handlers, bitten two grooms and broken through the safety fence around his yard.

He'd been a devil to groom judging by the shouts coming from the humans and had treated being tacked up the same way others prepare for war.

No, that was one to keep your distance from if there ever was one.

The big black Ahzzadel bared his teeth at Harlan as his rider moved up beside them, away from the earlier commotion.

The trias laid his ears back but still took the opportunity to bend down and grab a mouthful of a bush in passing; he relaxed better when his mouth was moving.

'Well, aren't ya a quiet one now,' the black stallion's rider chuckled.

Jhon had grabbed on to the black leather bridle when the noises had started, having anticipated trouble. Now he let go, giving the horse a few pats on the neck before he straightened out the large, blue blanket behind the saddle.

'Yar a good horse, aren't ya. I always said to me and mine. It's the quiet ones ya have ta watch,' he grinned at Sam.

Jhon clucked knowingly. 'Na need ta worry laddie. Ya'll see yer ole master and mistress soon enough.'

Seranthiem gave a polite nod. Not sure if Jhon was talking to him or the horse.

Harlan wasn't paying much attention. He'd turned his head to sniff at a passing bay, but, having decided it wasn't going to bite him, he was now content to ignore it and returned to surveying the surroundings.

While the small stallion rarely seemed to react to anything he was watching, he was always watching. He didn't bother about fighting. He let the bigger, badder horses fight amongst themselves; then, when they were tired, he could do as he pleased anyway and with a lot less fuss.

Now he carefully studied the lights, the buildings, the people, and, of course, the other horses, as the milling, churning hoard of bodies moved down the lane and down to the starting line for today's course.

He found himself quickening his pace, Sam content for now merely to guide him in the right direction.

Jhon took a moment to have a few short words with the silver-haired man just before the starting grid as Harlan insisted on stopping there anyway. He waved the hand that wasn't holding on to the reins casually.

'Ya better get back the stands boy, if ya mean to catch the run for watchin', don't wanna' miss anything, now do ya?'

Not having any idea of what the man meant, Seranthiem blinked a couple of times.

'Best of luck then. Take care out there. It would seem Ahzzadel's got an eye on you two now,' Sam replied politely, his eyes scanning the crowd with a calculating gaze.

The start was always dangerous. So many things could go wrong. Things he had no control over. Once they were away, the field would spread out and the worries would come in much smaller doses.

'Na need ta worrie laddie. We'll be right on careful out there. Too bad for us though, not only "normal" horses in this run today. Need to watch out for fangs an' horns ta.'

Up in the stands, Erina struggled to see what was going on. She'd have welcomed a box. To stand on or to stand in, she wasn't choosy. The better known stables had them. It was just her luck she was just starting out.

Mind you, she wasn't sure she'd have wanted one. It did single you out in the most obvious of ways.

Treee did much the same. He cut through the crowd like a steamer through churning waters — and the waters just parted for him too.

'How unfair.'

As such, it didn't take too long to get where he was going. It would have taken even less if there hadn't been so many people getting in the way. He managed to refrain from frowning at them but, right now, even that was taking quite a bit of an effort.

'Still half the field to load,' Erina commented as she leaned forwards on to the railing.

'Load?' Tom squinted down at the run. 'I don't see any gates?'

'It works as well as any other. I have no idea what all these expressions they throw around here actually mean. Well, most of them.' She put the light-weight binos to her eyes.

'Didn't expect so many,' Treee took in the sheer amount of souls present.

'Popular, I guess. Look, the officials are coming out. Any minute now.'

Seranthiem nudged Harlan forwards and winced. It had not been a good day and it looked like it was only getting worse.

Erina's voice wasn't the only grating pain around and thanks to him not paying attention to where he was going this was going to take more effort than usual.

How this was going to turn out he didn't know, but he wasn't exactly looking forward to finding out what Erina would say if it went badly.

In contrast, the atmosphere in the owners' section of the specially erected stand was relaxed and excited. Smiles and laughter mingled happily with the tinkling exchanges of glasses and plates for those who chose this time for a slight nibble.

CHAPTER SEVEN

Down on the field below, cookies of grass were being kicked up by steel-shod hooves as the host of horses stomped around behind the starting line.

Ahzzadel, his needle-like ears pinned, tossed his head. His mood hadn't improved a bit since this strange human had been heaped onto his back and what little remained of it was evaporating rapidly.

Nerves and tempers alike were beginning to flare up in pockets everywhere. Tight bundles of energy, like coiled corks, all but ready to shoot out of the bottle and into the chandelier, hitting two vases and a gnome before ending up in the ornamental duck pond.

None of them much cared for the small, bright bullet that was bouncing around among them like a loosened cannonball.

Neighs and shouts of protest followed Harlan's erratic progress through the mass.

Sam's hand remained soft. His balance graceful.

He caught sight of Jhon, who was trying to hold back his horse with only one hand, the other pulling at his goggles. Without them on, the sun must sting his eyes, Sam thought. Knowing the horn could go at any moment, he brushed an errant strand from his long, silvery hair out of the way. He hoped it wouldn't come loose during the race. Not even his eyes could see "through" such solid matter.

Echoes of metal and animal impacts travelled through the other sounds with unpleasant clangs as a large body struck one of the outposts. The mare next to the troublemaker was lifting his back legs threateningly as the other got too close.

It was spreading now — the tension. As if the racers weren't already strung like a couple of renaissance violins.

One of the riders, Remi, regarded it all quietly. The large, angular bay mare beneath him just stood there. She didn't as much as twitch while the insanity level around them kept rising.

She'd come to them as a sprinter. A very bad sprinter from a stable that had given up on her. She'd work herself up to a reasonable speed after a few hundred meters and then that was it; they couldn't get anything more out of her.

What they had never done was to try her long distance. Okay, so the horse wasn't photogenic, Remi thought. She didn't have great bloodlines or any of the "heart" that riders and owners referred to when bragging about their horses. What she did have was stamina. Seemingly endless reserves of stamina. The bay mare, once she'd reached her "cruising" speed, she just kept going, and going, and going.

And she didn't let things get to her either. He'd walked her past flapping sheets, brass bands, crowds, stampeding herds (although in that case "walking" was not what he'd been doing) and she wouldn't as much as flick an ear in their direction as long as she trusted her rider.

He'd looked about earlier. Remi wasn't familiar with the racing styles of all the entrants, but he doubted that there were any here who could match her for endurance. And with all this ruckus going on, so many of them were expending precious energy already, and the race hadn't even started yet. He rolled his tongue over his teeth, clicking disapprovingly.

Then, as the sun peeked out from behind one of the nimbus clouds, the sound of the starting horn rolled over them.

They were off!

As one, the whole host of horse-ish bodies threw themselves forward. A moment later they were followed by the members of the throng who had been dancing sideways or investigating a promising tuft of hollow bush.

Standing. Milling. Prancing. It didn't matter. They were swept along.

Pushed forwards by the sheer mass of bodies behind them. Knocked aside or generally run into; it forced them to move in the general direction out of simple desire not to get knocked over and trampled.

The break, as a wave releasing its energy upon the shore, thundered past the first marker, legs pumping rhythmically with that first burst of adrenalin.

Harlan snorted. He was being pushed and shoved from all directions and the dust from the earthy side of the starting line was filling the air.

With all the rain that had fallen the night before, it should have been muddy, but this wasn't your normal type of soil, and so it billowed up at even the slightest disturbance: a pack of horses running through it and you were lucky to see your hand in front of you.

That, of course, was why it had been placed there in the first place.

The horse just to Harlan's left put his teeth in his rump as he passed. The trias broke his stride, a displeased neigh escaping from his throat. Then the grey's rider was pulling at the reins, trying desperately to steer his mount away and free.

Struggling to get his mount to concentrate on running, they quickly dropped to the back of the rapidly expanding field.

'Well, we're not out of this yet,' Sam mumbled. Then promptly closed his mouth, for it filled with foul-tasting sand and dirt.[9]

Trying to get his bearings, he scanned the runners up ahead. Burying his head, bending as low as he could over the muscular neck, Sam clung to the powerful body as they surged over the first hill and approached the outskirts of the forest.

This first part of the race never had any obstacles. But once they passed into the woodlands, they were entering the race proper. And, having inspected the "course" earlier, it had been evident that the initial run through the forest was going to be a dark one. He could already see the runners up ahead disappearing into the shadows.

Great trees with trunks not even four grown men could have encircled towered above them. Their branches were full to the bursting with large, dark green leaves. Roots crawling over the ground.

---

[9] If he'd been an earthworm, he'd have thought the banquet had come early. But he wasn't. So, he didn't.

As they galloped past the first of the forest markers, the last light of the sun was already vanishing overhead as the crowns of the trees stretched out and intertwined above the path.

Beneath them it was murky; a musty scent of mull and lichen rising from the forest floor. Even the air seemed denser in here.

As they passed the next marker at speed, Seranthiem tried to meld himself to the horse's neck. He didn't want to get caught by a random branch somewhere.

Below him, muscles rippled under the sleek coat as Harlan's hooves pounded against the soft floor of the forest, crushing twigs and leaves beneath them.

He's barely slowed down from the first open stretch, zigging and zagging through the brown trunks like he'd been born for it, Sam thought.

For a moment, they were running head to head with a large chestnut gelding, fighting to be the first to reach the narrowing gap ahead. It didn't look wide enough for them to be able to pass through side by side so each was desperately trying to pull ahead.

Then the other horse dropped back, no longer being urged on; his rider lost to one of the branches that had narrowly missed knocking Jhon off on the training run they'd had yesterday.

They shot out of the forest and into the light. The blinding light.

Scenting the water beyond, Sam tried to steer Harlan to the left.

Instead of going momentarily blind, and subsequently getting dunked into the pond just beyond by a horse finding their emergency brakes, Sam knew exactly where he wanted to go. He guided them around the edge of the watery obstacle almost lazily, splashing through the shallows.

From behind him, came the sad cry of yet another rider getting unexpectedly unseated as they hit the depths of the pond without warning.

They were catching up.

Focusing ahead, Sam saw a clump of horses running together. Two of the three equines at the front were fighting for dominance, neither willing to yield, and neither willing to commit the extra power to pull past, there being a whole race left to run. The third was running, ears pinned, to escape from the nightmare coming up from behind, snapping and nipping at his hocks and rump.

Just coming up on a sharp bend around a set of large boulders, the black and gold racing blanket behind Sam rippled in the wind. He steered his mount closer to the outer side, having no wish to get his legs crushed against the solid wall of rock.

Harlan, on the other hand, seemed as intent as ever to go through the clump of horses the hard way, right through the middle. Tossing his head, he fought against the reins, his steps beginning to slide on the tall, damp grass.

Unlike Harlan, Sam knew that there was a set of very sharp, over ninety degree, turns coming up, and he wanted to be on the outside of the first one to have plenty of room to manoeuvre.

While Sam knew Harlan wasn't bothered by tight turns, he'd seen him being taken out for some barrel racing and pole bending just to loosen him up and keep him happy, this wasn't the same. A solid rock wall wasn't the same as an empty barrel, should you, well, barrel into it.

Not caring much for all the pushing and shoving going on around him, his rump still throbbing from earlier, Harlan bunched up. Sam tightened his grip. He didn't want to fall. Not here. Not now.

'They seem to do quite well,' Tom commented casually back in the stands.

'Only because most of the horses behind them are either slow, riderless, or taking an unauthorized lunch munch!' Erina snorted grimly.

She watched, hands gripping the rail until her knuckles turned white, feeling every turn in her stomach, every time Sam and Harlan disappeared from sight behind another boulder.

'There, I see 'em!'

'What? Where?'

Erina squinted at the huge screen hovering before the stands, nearly missing them as they were lost amongst a group throwing themselves through the great stone gate and onto the open plains beyond.

Suddenly having room to spread out, the mob of equines drifted apart.

Watching the horse and rider zigzag over the now open grassland imitation, Erina made a wry face. It was hard to tell from this distance if the somewhat erratic course the pair was setting was because they were still disagreeing on where to go or if Harlan was merely being his usual self.

One of the first things that Erina had noticed about her friend was that Harlan seemed to run in straight lines about as often as a pigeon attacked a bird of prey. He was always drifting left or right all over the place, needing to cover almost twice as much ground to get where he was going as other horses.

That might well be great if you were trying to avoid enemy fire. It wasn't quite so good when trying to get from A to B in the shortest possible amount of time. If only he could be convinced not to do this, she was certain that he'd have a very good chance at this game.

Now, as they flew over the first ridge, Sam tried to recall the layout of the course. What would be waiting for them beyond?

There were always a few surprises thrown into a race like this to shake it up a bit. While not lethal, except by sheer accident, sometimes those surprises could be quite startling. Especially if you were a horse.

Down below, there was a stream. Too wide and deep to be a brook, too small to be a river, the sides were filled with reeds.

Just as Harlan tightened himself for the jump across, two scarecrows popped up from beneath the water. Snorting, eyes white, the stallion kicked off much harder than intended, leaping nearly diagonally across the stream.

'Easy, easy, boy,' Sam tried to calm the horse as he dashed off. Maybe the dripping wet, soggy creatures didn't want to eat him. Maybe they did. He wasn't going to stay around to find out.

Sam tightened his grip on the reins. They needed to get away from the stream, not run alongside it or…

'Aaaaah!!'

Sam struggled to regain his balance as Harlan shied away from the birds erupting out of the water before him, dancing almost backwards to avoid being struck by the small, brown bodies as they launched themselves skyward.

'Ayarch! Quack! Quaarck!' they cried, their great wings striking against the water.

'Whoa, boy! Eaasy!'

The soft, mushy bottom of the river yielded beneath Harlan's hooves as they slipped and slid through the banks. Away. Away from these strange things. He needed to get away.

Despite a lifetime in the wild — or maybe because of it — Harlan cared little for unexpected surprises.

Sam managed to hold on as they struck out for the shore and a, thankfully, mostly flat expanse of grass extending past the assembly all the way past the finish line.

Only the last leg left now.

First, they needed to get to the top of the last hill though.

Harlan collected his legs and settled down to a free gallop as Sam urged him forwards. Head thrust out, mane and tail streaming, his hooves beat out their 'thud, thud, thud' against the grass, still moist from the morning's rain.

The stands were coming up ahead.

So were a scattered number of equines. They were catching them up.

Breathing heavily, Harlan threw them across the finish line, having almost, but not quite, caught up to the big black.

Already waiting for them was the slithery grey that had bit him earlier. Snarling and snapping, the nightmare was again battling against his handlers. An eye, yellow and cold, shot a poisonous look in Harlan's direction.

Then, it was all over.

Or was it?

And so, the official grades having been awarded, points distributed, and the winners cheered, there were only a few things left to do for the day. Amongst them came the records.

'Does he have any problem with flashes?' the young recorder wanted to know.

'Not that I know of,' Erina answered.

She fussed over tying the lead to the halter while the young horse affectionately tried to eat her hair. His human was back. He was happy. She couldn't say *she* was happy about this.

She didn't care much for this whole "recording" either. But apparently it was a recognized part of the aftermath of the race. Maybe it made sense to some, but Erina couldn't see what all the fuss was about. In a few years' time, not one would probably remember it anyway.

'Good to hear. Some of them can get a bit excited,' the recorder said, finishing the adjustments to his equipment and peering into the viewer, trying to get the light just right.

Most of the equipment was automated, but he liked doing things the old-fashioned way even so.

'Move a little closer, please,' the recorder instructed Sam, who, reluctantly, moved into the frame.

He, at least, didn't seem to like this idea any better than she did, Erina noted.

'Harlie, behave yourself,' she cautioned Harlan. Trying to sound stern, she failed dismally.

It was hard to be harsh with the young stallion. He generally didn't get up to mischief, much, and when he was caught doing something that he shouldn't have done, he generally just stood there radiating innocence.

It would have been like kicking the biggest, little puppy in the world — albeit a puppy that reached to your head and weighed in at several hundred pounds. Sometimes Erina wondered if he thought that his two-legged herd members were horses too? He certainly acted like it at times.

The white sheet hanging behind them, separating the main arena from the photo shoots, didn't seem to bother him at all. She hadn't expected it to, but you never knew, with new places and all that.

'Ok, we're good to go.'

'Right.'

Click!

Flash!

Harlan shied back from the sudden light! Into the sheet behind him he bumped, throwing his head, threatening to tear it from its temporary fastenings.

'Haaarlan!'

CHAPTER EIGHT

The next few days, amongst the hectic hustle and bustle of departing runners and caretakers, Erina and Harlan enjoyed long rides in the extensive grounds (avoiding those areas closed off due to other races) and merely relaxed and enjoying themselves.

She might have enjoyed these little outings a bit more if Sam hadn't had to accompany her every time she took Harlan out. "Had to" being the operative word.

'You are not accredited to ride on these lands,' Sam had stated. And no matter how much she'd argued, that had been that.

In the paddocks, or even fenced-in fields, it was fine. But if she wanted to go out beyond that, she needed a certified companion. No matter her grumbling, that was a fact she couldn't escape. Not if she wanted to be allowed to return.

Sometimes she wondered if it was worth the annoyance.

That first day, Erina had felt like sneaking out in the middle of the night, like some midnight raider, and go for a joyride.

'So much for liberty,' she'd gripe every time they saddled up.

It'd take at least half-an-hour before the sheer annoyance at it all began to soften. Sam had learnt not to speak to her before then.

Not that he and Wave Rock were bad company. At least, he didn't think they were. No one had ever complained about them before.

Unlike their riders, Harlan and Rocky were already becoming fast friends. They enjoyed these little trips. Probably far more than the people they carried.

'The transport is scheduled for tomorrow,' Erina said during one of these rides, checking her diom to make sure she had the dates right. 'Then we'll be out of your hair.'

'I'll set out all the equipment for them, my lady. Will you be accompanying them?'

'Yes,' Erina rubbed at her eyes. 'It's easier to get to by horseback.'

'This stable. I was not aware there were inaccessible locations on this world. It must be located far from … everything.'

Erina couldn't help but laugh. 'You have NO idea.'

The cries of distressed horses echoed through the fog and the heavy darkness of the night. Through the walls of the old stable and the new, they came, mingling in the courtyard to create a cacophony of unprecedented proportions.

Even those of a less nervous disposition were kicking in their boxes, their eyes rolling.

Despite the unusual orchestra of the entire wing, it didn't manage to drown out the shrill screams of the dark grey nightmare. Nor did they hide the sounds of a loose box being demolished.

Sharp hooves, kicks, even teeth, bit into the semblance wood, tearing out chunks and spitting them aside.

There was already blood splatter dripping from Ahzzadel's mouth — from where he'd literally chewed his way out of his enclosure. He didn't seem to notice. Working in a manic frenzy, he destroyed what was left of the stable door.

He hadn't more than finished tearing it down before a heavy body launched itself from within the shadows, straight at his neck.

Harlan's teeth clamped down, as Ahzzadel reared to get away, screaming in anger.

He couldn't hold on long. Soon, too soon, the nightmare broke free.

They charged each other again. Slashing claws met fierce kicks. Fangs snapped. Teeth chomped.

The two circled each other in a macabre dance of menace and violence.

'What the hell is going on?' the head groom appeared out of his quarters, summoned by the night officer. He tried desperately to tuck in his shirt as he was running.

'It's gone crazy sir, absolutely bonkers!'

The head groom resisted the urge to roll his eyes. The night officer's continued insistence to always understate everything had been getting on his nerves more than usual lately.

'One of the nightmares then?' he shouted over the din.

'It's that bloody snake,' the night officer yelled back. 'He's tearing the guest stables apart.' He was breathing hard, having already run all the way to the head groom's quarters, and now having to run all the way back, his words were coming out alongside short bursts of air.

Dressing gowns pulled over sleepwear mingled with mussed hair and tangled trousers. Now, other people were tripping over the low stairs as they rushed towards the noise — hoping that the stables weren't on fire.

By now the walls of the loose box had been stripped down to its building blocks in places. The semblance wood from there, cut and chewed, dripping with a mixture of saliva and blood, lay scattered over what remained of the bedding. Even the ground outside had had pits dug into it from the battle.

The wooden bars had been kicked, bitten, and generally abused until they'd nearly torn apart. Several bits of other doors were already sporting gaping holes. If they'd been taking a systematic and focused attack they'd have been torn to shreds already. It was mere luck that had had them miss so much of the damage.

From up ahead came the sounds of large bodies slamming against walls and doors indiscriminately. Again and again came the screams.

Making contact with a stone wall, the impact sent jarring shudders all through Harlan's body. Sharp stone flakes shot off in all directions, searing his already injured legs and belly.

If Harlan noticed the pain from his new wounds any more than he noticed the cuts and abrasions on his otherwise so sensitive muzzle or the corresponding ones on his gums, he didn't show it.

He barely even realized that hot blood from several angry, serrated wound flowed down his front legs. It was forming a sticky mess on his coat, smearing the attacking nightmare in red as they crashed.

If anything, the blood worked Ahzzadel into even more of a frenzy. All he knew was the burning, searing pain in his mind. A white hot light so bright it was blinding. Hatred. Pure, unadulterated hatred gleamed in his burning, yellow, reptile-like eyes.

The other was everywhere. No matter where he turned it was already there. Crushing. Pulling. Screeching. Tormenting. But even with conscious thought long since lost, the stallion's night was still only in its infancy.

'Noo! Don't open the gates!' The head groom screamed loudly at some men pulling at the locks. 'Block the area!'

For a moment, Harlan stumbled, finding only empty space before him. Then his failing eyesight locked-on to the grey. He pulled himself together and, as the other charged, slammed into him, hard.

The force was enough to knock both of them off their feet.

Ahzzadel was quickest back on his. But now there were all these other targets around. Smaller, easier targets that didn't kick your knees to kingdom-come. He lunged at the nearest one.

Arriving at a run, Erina was just in time to hear the man shriek as the nightmare's fangs locked around his arm, tearing through jacket, skin, and bone. Ahzzadel shook him from side to side, shredding the exposed limb.

'Shoot him. SHOOT HIM!!'

The man screamed as the arm was torn apart. The last he saw were the gaping, salivating jaws stretched wide, bearing down on his head.

The grey nightmare reared, pawing at the air.

The men had managed to block off the access routes to the yard with large, bulky items: mostly vehicles of sorts. Things that had been able to be moved in a hurry.

That didn't help the four-legged residents frantically trying to escape from the sounds of carnage.

'What are you doing?' Erina shouted through the din. 'Don't just stand there!'

'The tranqs aren't working!' One of the men called out.

'I can see that!'

'We can ALL see that!'

'Well DO something!'

'Get Castle. Quick. He'll have something stronger.'

'What about *my* horse?' Erina shook the man closest. 'He'll be torn to pieces by the time they get back!'

'Nothing to be done, madam,' he protested and tried desperately to back away as Ahzzadel slipped and barrelled into the wall just in front of him.

Hisses erupted together with his snarls as he struggled to get his legs together. He lunged at the nearest warm body, red dancing in front of his eyes, screeching as the man scrambled out of range just in time.

Erina's eyes took in the scene. The yard had been almost completely blocked off now. The men were retreating behind their barricades. With no more moving targets, the slimy snake would go after Harlan.

Her hands clenched.

'If you're not going to do something about this, I am!' she growled.

'WAIT! You can't— '

Erina slipped through the last barricade as they pushed it into place. They were all shouting now. Ahzzadel was trapped.

He didn't like being trapped. Needle-like ears pinned, he raced around the enclosure. Catching Erina in the corner of his eyes, he whirled around, kicking up even more dust, and made straight for her.

Her eyes narrowed. A grim line appeared where her lips had been. 'Come on, you pickled bastard.'

'HEY! YOU CAN'T— '

Erina pulled something free. The metal glimmered.

There was that moment when nightmare and human collided. Ahzzadel screamed in rage. Harlan clamped his teeth into a back leg.

Something heavy thudded to the ground. It added to the vision-impairing particles already intoxicating the air.

Then, there was silence.

CHAPTER NINE

It was hard to imagine how fast time moved when you were having your hands full, Erina thought. Still, things had quieted down — even if it had taken an unbelievable amount of effort to get there.

Had it really been several days already?

'There, there now,' Erina loosened the girth holding on the special blanket they'd been given by the attending physician.

Harlan's head hung, his muzzle almost touching the ground. It hovered over a bucket of strong mush. But he wasn't eating it.

Rubbing one of the stallion's back legs, Seranthiem reached behind him, selecting a new piece of cloth. Grabbing a bottle next to the cloth pile, he dabbed some brown liquid onto the fabric, then returned his attention to the leg.

Erina stroked the horse's cheek.

'There, there, I won't let any of those stupid people hurt you, promise,' Erina spoke soothingly.

'Does this happen often?'

Seranthiem paused, his hand about to move on to the next leg. 'I would like to say it is a rare event,' he said, guessing at what she was asking. 'But—'

'It's not, is it?'

'I'm sorry, my lady.'

'What d'you think?' Erina almost snarled, before remembering where she was and forcing herself to speak calmly.

'I'm sorry, I didn't mean to...'

'Whatever,' Erina mumbled crossly.

She looked so miserable that Sam took pity on her. 'There is no need for concern. Harlan will recover fine. The Court's physicians are among the best,' he tried to reassure her.

'Yes…well…' Erina hesitated. 'It's not been the best of experiences, over-all. It's easier when you can just hit things.'

Sam wisely chose to change the subject.

'Ahem… I profess I have been quite curious for some time of this place that you always refer to only as "the Valley." From what little description I have heard, I have failed to place it?'

This earned a small chuckle from the young woman. She rose from where she was sitting, giving Harlan a final scratch under his chin.

'I'd have been very surprised if you had.'

Harlan turned his head, trying to munch on Erina's jacket collar.

'Well, see who's finally decided to join us,' she rubbed his forehead. 'Feeling better, boy?'

Over her shoulder, she could see Sam looking a little perplexed. She couldn't help but smile a little. It was a rare thing to see such an expression on him. He was such a know-it-all. There was something terribly enjoyable about causing that…

🐎🐎🐎

'There isn't anything there,' Seranthiem insisted.

He was bent over an old-fashioned map on the table.

'I just told you there is,' Erina retorted stubbornly. She ought to know. After all, she lived there.

'However, the question remains. Should I be willing to accept your word in this matter or should I put faith in the scientific ordinance survey?' Sam waved a digital copy into being.

'Can't help you with that one,' Erina shrugged.

Sam mulled over those words for some time before continuing. At least it looked like he did, as he paced back and forth in front of the map hovering in the centre of the conference room.

'It sounds quite unlikely that something like this would have been continuously missed ever since this world was first settled.'

'You mean, *crashed into*,' Erina snorted.

Seranthiem waved a hand dismissingly. 'Mere semantics in this case.'

Erina shrugged non-committally. 'I didn't think so either … once I figured out where I was anyway.' She pursed her lips, thinking. 'I checked though once I got back to civilization. Even the shuttle patterns go around it. Even when on the map they're shown to be straight lines. People notice it, they just don't see it.'

'That sounds equally implausible,' Sam stated calmly.

'Don't ask me to explain it, I'm no expert. Maybe it's got some sort of perception filter thingy on it?'

'The theories behind such a device have never been scientifically proven,' Sam countered. 'And even if such technology did exist, essentially cloaking miles upon miles of rock rising up into the sky would need quite a power behind it to function, assuming it operated at that scale at all.'

'Proven by us you mean. Who says that any that were here before us had the same problem?'

'There's never been any clear evidence for sentient life having evolved on this world. Indeed, for such a world it has always been somewhat deficient in the abundant life you would expect, if you exclude vegetation,' Sam continued, ignoring Erina's interruption.

'Just because no one's *found* any before doesn't mean there weren't any,' Erina countered stubbornly.

'It is without doubt extensively researched, both at the time and continuously since then— Wait … did you say *before*, my lady?'

Seranthiem blinked, stopped his pacing and turned to face her directly.

Erina, on the other hand, regarded him with an unfazed, unmoving expression.

'Yes, yes I did. And it's no surprise no one's found any, even I remember enough of my geology lessons to figure out that everything points to this place having undergone some sort of really big disaster in the past. Big enough to wipe almost all life from it, with just enough lucky ones somehow escaping, or maybe being impervious to whatever happened. It just so happens that no one's looked in the right place yet for anything more sensible.'

'It is true that a cataclysmic event of truly epic proportions must have occurred in the planet's past to explain the features of it that we have come to take for granted. But what you propose is quite preposterous. Even if I was to believe you — believe that this place exists — the estimates of its height would place the plateau somewhere in the upper stratosphere — and that *IS* impossible.'

Seranthiem gestured somewhat agitatedly around the room. 'The fact that the temperature would be beyond cold would be the least of your troubles.'

'Oh, so something a little bit bigger than just a perception filter then,' Erina mused. 'Maybe to those that made it there wasn't much of a difference?'

'*Made*?' Sam threw her a contemptuous glare. 'My lady, we are talking about something that would need nothing less than a tectonic event of unimaginable proportions to be even possible. Assuming it is. And there's nothing like that on the rest of the planet. That it would be the sole survivor of such a single event … that only it would have been formed in the first place, is even less than likely.'

'How d'you know? No one knew this place existed until I found it. That's kind of the point.' Erina thought for a moment while drumming her fingers on the desk. 'Or maybe they found it and just couldn't get back again? It's not like it's got a revolving door. Most people still won't see it no matter what.'

The young woman made a face. She pulled out a padded chair to sit on. This was beginning to remind her of the arguments she used to have with her professors at the academy. She'd never been very good at getting her point across to them either.

On the other hand, unlike them, Seranthiem *was* still listening. Okay, so at the moment he was probably thinking she was a complete loony, but he still seemed fascinated by the idea and fascinated enough to at least consider the possibility that she was telling the truth.

Suddenly, she leaned forward and grinned triumphantly. 'Like the one they say happened then,' Erina grinned at him in return.

'No! Yes. I don't know. Maybe.'

Seranthiem started pacing again, thought better of it, and looked around for another chair. There were plenty around, this room normally being used for conferences. He picked up one of them and moved it closer to the table.

Sitting down, rubbing at his temples with thumb and forefingers, Sam continued. 'This isn't really my field at all,' he admitted reluctantly.

'It's no one's field,' Erina retorted, using her "I'm serious" voice. 'Think about it. No one knows anything about it yet.'

'Very well. Say for one moment that I suspend my disbelief. What exactly is it that I would be believing?'

'You mean what's up there,' Erina grinned at him.

'Possibly.'

If he was curious, he was doing a really good impression of not being more than just casually interested. Erina just shrugged. She sure seemed to be doing a whole lot of work in this conversation.

'As far as I can tell, it's a whole separate little world. The rules are the same as down here … most of the time.'

Sam raised a questing eyebrow at this description and Erina had the decency to look embarrassed. '*Only* most?'

'Well, that's the best description I can think of anyway. It's certainly what it feels like,' she leaned back crossing her arms defensively.

'A whole, completely isolated ecosystem then? Would not the birds visit?'

'Sam, you just pointed out five minutes ago that it's way too high for that. It's way too high for *anything*,' Erina shook her head, trying to resist the urge to laugh at him.

'But couldn't they come in the same way you did?' Sam queried.

'I don't know,' Erina admitted. 'Maybe that was an accident or something. Maybe I found a way in that no one else has, so I could get out again *and* remember the whole thing. Or maybe the rules changed. They do that — a lot. Anyway, even animals down here don't seem to "see" it.'

'I would imagine the surrounding atmosphere is hardly conducive for a temperate climate,' Sam said. 'How high did you say the plateau is?'

'Can't measure it, remember? But it's kind of amazing no spaceships just crash right into it.'

'So, quite tall then.'

'But it's not just isolated — it's old. I mean really, really old. A lot of the trees and such look a bit similar to what we've got here, but the animals certainly don't. There's a lot that isn't anything like what we've got, even if you ignore everything that came with the first settlers. And there are *buildings*. Well,' Erina coughed delicately, 'there's the *remains* of buildings at least. Ruins. Scattered all about the place. Most of the ones I've seen are just bits of rubble, but there's interesting bits too.'

'There were people there once?' Sam's grey eyes bore into her.

'Well, duh,' Erina rolled her eyes at him. 'You don't think they built themselves, do you?'

Seranthiem gave her a stern look and then selected his next words with care. 'I do not think anything about it until I have witnessed it with my own eyes,' he said.

'Oh.'

'Yet, assuming that you are indeed telling the truth, if the people are gone…?' he gave her a questioning glance waiting to see if she would confirm what he believed to hold true.

'Oh, they're gone alright. No trace whatsoever. Must have been ages ago too.'

Sam nodded distractedly, as if this merely confirmed what he'd already suspected.

'Then what is protecting this haven now?' he queried, a graceful frown adorning his otherwise flawless brow. 'A completely independent ecosystem of this size, untouchable to anything from the outside and vice-versa, shouldn't be sustainable over the amount of time we are talking about. And if it is shielded from the surrounding atmosphere somehow, as suggested by the fact that it's not frozen solid, how does it rain?'

'Obviously it doesn't know it shouldn't be there. It seems to be doing well enough for itself,' Erina said, waving away his arguments with a casual flick of her hand.

'That is not an answer,' Sam frowned. 'If there was a people that had the kind of power that would protect this phenomenon through what troubled times they faced, why did they choose such a small area? But then, if it *were* them, how come it is still functioning long after they're gone? Either they set in motion something that was perpetual or something else was behind it from the beginning.'

'Well, you can't exactly go and ask them, now can you?' Erina's voice dripped with sarcasm.

She was getting increasingly annoyed with the conversation. The thing was there, wasn't it? It wasn't as if there was much of a point going around constructing hypotheses about how it wasn't, since it, obviously, was.

Not that Sam seemed to have noticed the dropping temperature of their little talk. He continued as if he hadn't heard that last little outburst at all.

'So, whatever it is that is powering this phenomenon must be weakening,' Sam speculated.

'Does it really matter? Do you want to see it or don't you? I could do with another set of hands around the place, and you seem to handle yourself well enough.'

'Perhaps you are right. But I would like to see this place for myself,' Sam said, 'before deciding.' He added in an, 'assuming it exists,' a moment later.

'Works for me,' Erina beamed. 'Harlan should be well recovered in a few days. We can go almost right away.'

Sam made a small bow in her direction. 'I regret to inform you it will take a little longer than that to set my affairs in order, my lady. Perhaps, if you were to provide me with directions, I can follow later?'

'Directions to a place that can't be found? Yeah, I can see that going real well,' Erina rolled her eyes at him. 'Oh, alright. We'll try it your way first. Just don't come crying to me if it doesn't work.'

🐉 🐉 🐉

And so, several weeks after Erina had already left, Sam walked his horse off the transport.

Wave Rock pawed a bit at the loose ground. It wasn't quite sand here, not yet.

'Sure you wanna head out into that?' the transport's driver nodded at the stony desert.

'Affirmative,' Sam nodded.

Shaking his head in disbelief, the driver revved up the transport and was soon little more than a dot on the horizon.

Taking a deep breath, Sam drew in all the scents in the air. It was early morning and already it had a burning flavour as it touched his tongue. Yet Erina had assured him that "most" of the Valley was actually temperate in climate.

"Most" seemed to be a word she used a lot when describing the place. He took another breath. Soon he would see for himself and then he'd know.

'It would seem we have fallen in with a strange crowd, Wave,' he said as he swung into the saddle. 'We should be careful.'

And with that, he nudged the buckskin forwards.

Many hours later and the sun was causing sweat to trickle down Wave Rock's coat. It had been growing hotter and hotter until it even became hard to breathe — causing Sam to seriously consider turning back. Then, it changed.

It wasn't a sudden change, but, when looking around, it didn't make any sense to him.

Below him Wave Rock pawed nervously at the ground. Each strike sent up a new cloud of incredibly minute and fine dust particles.

The air here smelled wrong and what little of the sky you could see was now covered in unfriendly looking clouds. The rocks and cliffs they were passing were jagged and sharp to the touch and black as sin. They loomed out of the silken sand dust like ancient piranhas fossilized in the moment they'd broken surface into this hostile world. Wave Rock was already sporting several small cuts where he'd brushed against the sharp stone.

Beneath his hooves the ground was smooth and gentle, but oh-so-delicate. Every step he took, if he even as much as shifted his weight or breathed in the wrong direction, the ground would give birth to a million small clouds that'd rise and swirl and generally make themselves a nuisance.

They'd then hang in the air, seemingly for an eternity, before casually drifting back down long after the travellers were gone from sight and the original memory of their disturbance lost.

It'd get in your hair, that dust. It'd get in your eyes. Under your shirt. It'd wriggle its way into all those tiny places and crevices you had never paid attention to before; to say nothing about what it did to your nose and mouth.

And that was just the beginning.

'This doesn't match any known formations,' Sam told his horse. 'And according to the map, *this shouldn't even be here.*'

The stallion cast his eyes over the landscape — the bits of it that were visible anyway — and then looked down at his feet.

It'd be nice if the ground stayed put. But even though there wasn't as much as a gust of wind, not a single huff, there was still enough. The ground was in constant motion — especially the layer at the very top, which seeped and drifted like the offspring of a chance mating between a heavy mist and a windy day at the beach.

Maybe it wasn't even the wind that was doing it. What did he know? But it'd be nice if he could *see* his hooves, now that you mentioned it.

Because of the dust, both Wave Rock and Seranthiem now travelled enshrouded in a semi-hazed cloud; a slightly less dense patch of moving rock than the ground beneath them.

Dark shapes would appear and disappear around them as they moved forwards, drifting in and out of focus as the dust swallowed them. At least Sam *hoped* they were moving forwards. It was nearly impossible to tell and he didn't think it'd be a good place to start going around in circles.[10]

'Whoa, Wave,' Sam said and pulled them to a stop.

Sam was trying to read the map he'd brought along and it was difficult to concentrate as it was. Of course, it wasn't much of a map, he admitted. The hand-drawn scribbles bore the distinct smudged inkiness that came out of trying to use a fountain pen on paper that disagreed with it. And what wasn't smudged was so faded it was ridiculous. How was he supposed to use this thing? By now it could have given directions to either of the four moons for all he knew.

It would have been so much handier to just enter the coordinates into his diom. But when he'd suggested such, back then, the lady had merely laughed and told him he'd understand when he got there.

There had been things written on the piece of paper, but Sam only knew that because he remembered that was what the half-blotted patches were, what

---

[10] Another thing it lacked was someone suspicious-looking to stop and ask for directions.

was left of them. Not even he would have stood a chance at making them out now, not without some very specialized equipment, the likes of which he had, understandably, neglected to add to his travelling kit when first setting out.

It had been hard enough trying to make out what they had meant the first time he'd read them. Though that was mostly because he hadn't thought they'd made any sense.

Thinking back, the instructions seemed on par with the old "take a right at the third star on the left and straight on 'til morning." They were clearly not meant to make sense in the first place in his opinion, as if he wasn't already beginning to have serious doubts about this whole idea altogether even *without* that to add to his troubles.

Sam's eyes flicked between the "map" and the surrounding environment. A small sigh escaped from the scarf tied over his nose and mouth, and he carefully folded the piece of paper and stuffed it back into a pocket.

Wave Rock's nostrils flared as he offered a low 'harrumph,' signalling his displeasure at their current predicament.

'There, there now,' Sam comforted his horse, his voice muffled by the scarf that he'd tied on tightly.

He gave the unhappy buckskin stallion an encouraging pat on the neck and instantly wished he hadn't. It raised another small cloud of tiny debris only too happy to join their fellows that were already dancing their attendance on the pair.

'Great,' Sam muttered. 'As if things couldn't get any worse.'

He'd forgotten that they were both covered in the minute dust. He couldn't believe that had slipped his mind; they were absolutely covered, making them look like a small portable version of the ground.

Sam wondered if there were any nook or cranny somewhere where it hadn't gotten into. Any surface it hadn't covered? A hermetically sealed one, perhaps, but somehow, he doubted that there was one around here.

When they got out of here, he was going to have a long, serious wash as soon as possible, followed by a nice, cold bath. Actually, he thought, he'd better make that *several* serious washes: him and horse alike.

The only good thing about it was that, if they stood still, they blended in with the landscape. Not even a master chameleon could have done better. That left them almost invisible to any predators — assuming that anything hunting out here that relied on sight hadn't starved to death long ago.

Sam cast a glance around him. He couldn't imagine what could possibly be desperate enough to try to survive out here long-term. Probably something unexpected if he knew this world right. It was almost certain to involve lots of teeth or possibly mandibles. That was even worse. He tried not to think about it; he'd hate to lose his horse.

When they moved, on the other hand, it was like travelling with your own advertising agency; one which kept calling out "Dinner Here! Dinner Here! Dinner to go!" in a type of repetitive, and very soon annoying, jingle.

'We better get out of this soon,' he said trying not to cough. 'This is not somewhere I'd care to spend the night.'

Had they'd taken a wrong turn somewhere? It was possible. All these rocks looked pretty much alike if you ever saw them at all.

'Remind me again why I took this job?' Sam muttered darkly under his breath.

If he'd expected any sympathy from his, normally buckskin, horse, he would have been sadly disappointed.

As yet another hour passed, the sand dust finally began to recede, giving way to what Sam thought of as a slightly more normal world.

Instead of the pale, almost translucent, dust and sharp, black rocks, they were now seeing an increasing amount of red stone dotting the landscape here and there.

Unlike the jagged features of the previous stone, these were worn smooth, undulating in what looked like waves with their fine pattern of different coloured layers. Some sort of sedimentary rock, Sam figured. It was actually quite pretty, if he'd been in the mood for sightseeing.

The earth beneath them was getting firmer as well, and soon the horse's hooves were clattering over a cracked, but definitely solid, surface. Every step, every strike of hoof against stone and a small echo would ring along the walls that had risen to increasingly impressive heights around them.

Soon, they were surrounded by walls of red rock. Wavy red rocks. He thought it looked a bit as if a red sea had suddenly been frozen mid-wave and something had carved its way through them, creating a narrow canyon with walls as smooth as silk. Smooth to look at that was. He didn't test it to the touch.

Still, Sam thought, whatever it was, it was less a nuisance than the dust. They could breathe again now, even if the echo did ring unpleasantly in his sensitive ears…

At times, the rock walls around them curved; one of them would bend over the other so much that they nearly blocked out the sunlight. But most of the time they were making their way through an increasingly deep, but narrow, canyon.

Once they'd gotten used to sounds again, after that muffled experience out in the Sand Sea, they picked up the pace.

At least, Sam assumed it was the Sand Sea, as that was what it was called on all the maps he'd ever seen of the area. Still, he didn't recall any mentions of the sand being as fine or of those peculiar black rocks that'd crumble as you touched them even as they cut you.

Also, when he'd first set out, it had been a perfectly normal desert; or the outskirts of a desert anyway. The Sand Sea wasn't considered to be very big, quite the contrary. Most people stayed away from it though; there was just something about the place…

Sam had consulted the sad excuse for a map again before entering the canyon, and he guessed they didn't have far to go before they got into the "Valley."

Again, he had the same reluctance to go on, before finally shaking it off and moving forwards. It had been the same several times — but at least now that he was almost there, it was easier to decide to keep going. He had no interest in going back through the strange desert so soon. If nothing else, he was running low on supplies.

It had been a different matter the first couple of weeks after the High Fyelds' horse and owner had departed for their home and he'd started out several times only to change his mind and go back.

That was still a bit of a mystery he had to admit. He hadn't thought that there was a valley at the coordinates that Erina had pointed out on the survey map. In fact, neither did the survey map.

On that map, so painstakingly researched and cross-checked by several generations of cartographers, the whole area she indicated was labelled as the Sand Sea with one border running right along the side of the Eastern Sea. He'd always wondered who had thought that up. If they'd been named by the same person, they were obviously someone lacking in terms of imagination.

Also, Sam thought, this place he was going to was supposedly located on high grounds. *Very* high grounds. But he hadn't been moving upwards any more than was usual for this area. So how did that work?

Now, survey maps didn't go about just randomly displacing entire landmarks — to say nothing about a few mountain ranges, no matter how small — and Sam had been busy kicking himself for going along with this whole idea.

But she'd been very convincing. He had to give her that. If he had to be honest, she at least seemed to have been pretty certain that it was there.

'So are deluded fools, Sammi,' Seranthiem reminded himself.

Thinking back to that conversation in the conference room now served only to put Sam on edge. Was he beyond foolish for going along with this insane idea? Or perhaps he had just been suffering from a momentary lapse of sanity at the time when he'd agreed to come?

Then, why hadn't he just backed out of the whole thing? Turned around and gone home? What did he have to lose, really? Except some dignity…

Even so, the very idea tugged at him. It wouldn't leave him; always being at the back of his mind every waking hour since he'd first heard about it. He didn't know what it was, or why, but he knew he just had to know if it was true or not.

And now, the world of ochre was coming to an end. Just up above, there was a sliver of blue. Soon, a blue sky opened up above him.

Sam urged Wave Rock into a trot. Small pebbles, dislodged from above, scattered somewhere behind them.

Wave Rock tossed his head, pulling at the reins. His steps were getting faster and much, much more staccato.

'Easy,' Sam called out, taken off guard by the unexpected movement.

The stallion snorted. His nostrils flared and he kept moving his head up, and up. His eyes rolled.

'What's the matter,' Sam asked. His eyes scanned their surroundings. He couldn't see anything out of the ordinary. But he knew his horse. He wouldn't be acting up like this for no reason.

Sam took a tighter hold on the reins with his left hand. His right hand moved down, just below the saddle, and there his fingers curled around a familiar, and right now comforting, shape. He'd spent too much time and effort training his horse. He had no intention of losing him to some imaginary evil.

Under him the buckskin danced nervously, almost moving sideways at times.

Then he saw it.

It was just a glimpse: a dark shadow against the sky at the top of the cliff around them.

It looked like a horse, Sam thought. So, they had other equines here. If Erina was telling the truth, and it was beginning to look as if she was, equines wouldn't be the only thing he might encounter here.

A few moments went by occupied by nothing but the sounds of their breathing. When nothing appeared, he touched his heels gently to the horse's flanks and they moved forward cautiously.

It wasn't long before Sam caught another glimpse of the dark, lithe body. It was keeping pace with them, then it sped up, disappearing somewhere ahead.

'You utter moron!' Sam cussed under his breath. 'You of all people should have known better!'

Sam shifted in the saddle and sniffed the air experimentally. It smelled strange and unfamiliar. Neither were particularly good things, not if said something came equipped with a large number of teeth and claws, or, worse, a nasty disposition.

Not that Sam usually had much trouble in that department, largely because he had sense enough not to get involved in situations like that in the first place.

Some were harder than others to avoid; for instance, mosquitoes or gnats, or those nasty little things that dropped down on you when you walked past or hitched a ride should your feet wander too close and they were feeling hungry. To be apprehensive you had to have something to be apprehensive with in the first place.

Most animals on this world kept their distance from people. Okay, maybe some, like the notoriously bad tempered fungit, didn't — not if you got too close. He remembered vividly being chased through some woods by a whole pack when he'd been little, after having wandered straight into the glade they'd called home. He still had some of the teeth marks...

Sam smiled even as he continuously let his eyes dart from one sight to another. Like so many others before him, some lessons had to be learnt the hard way.

A tiny knot was growing between his shoulder blades.

He caught another glimpse of the creature just as they left the canyon, but then everything opened up, and the Valley lay before them. A lithe black shadow darting to one side, into the sun, then out of sight.

'What was that?' Sam asked himself. 'I hope it doesn't come any closer.'

It had seemed big and black. It seemed to be able to move quietly, even cautiously, and it didn't make much noises that he could hear.

He kept watching where it had disappeared. Wave Rock didn't seem to feel it was gone. And, quite honestly, neither did he.

Having kept a careful eye behind and above them, Sam now turned his attention forwards to inspect what he'd ridden into. He was wondering if this little trip was going to have been worth his time.

A small gasp escaped from his lips as his eyes widened.

Now looking upon it in full for the first time … he realized that looking upon it in full was actually the last thing he was doing.

Stretched out before him as far as the eye could see was... was... No, mere words just couldn't describe it.

'This is *no* valley!'

Seranthiem breathed out slowly. He hadn't even realized he'd been holding his breath.

Taking a moment to just stand there, taking it all in, he let his gaze sweep across the land that now lay before him. It was *nothing* like what he'd just left behind or anything like what he'd imagined.

When someone said "valley," he'd thought of something small and snug between maybe two outcroppings of mountains. But here...

There was grass, lots and lots of grass, disappearing into the distance. Even from here he could imagine the green canvas rippling gently as it was caressed by the wind.

From the flatlands to the rolling hills, until it disappeared under a canopy of woods and forests that hugged the mountains, was an emerald carpet. It was green below where Wave Rock stood too, but it wasn't grass. Were those tree crowns? That shifted the perspective somewhat.

Sam realized that he must be standing on some sort of outcrop, way above ground level. For the treetops belonged to the edge of a thin strip of forest that had climbed its way all the way up the ridge to the pass he'd just emerged from.

They had a rugged, gnarly look to them but, when moving a bit closer to the edge, he realized that they must be quite tall to reach all the way up here. It was a good thing he hadn't just tried to walk out onto that.

Here and there were the scattered bushes and the odd clump of that tall grass that lived on the edge where no other grass dared grow, more ochre and umber than actual green.

Otherwise, there wasn't much up here where he was, except the red rocky cliffs that rose almost vertically behind him on either side of the narrow canyon and the smattering of stones and gravel that you'd expect in such places.

Blinking a couple of times, to make sure he wasn't seeing things, there were diffuse shapes clinging to the horizon, either horizons, some albeit further and more hazier looking than others.

And towering above them on the northern side was a majestic set of peaks reaching so high that it was difficult to imagine something so tall even though it was right there in front of you. You blinked just to make sure and, yes, it was still there. It really was that tall.

Sam wondered *how* high it must be to be so far away and still dominate the skyline. To call it "huge" would have been doing it no favours.

'That thing's a right old monster.' He shaded his eyes trying to get a clearer picture. Sam took out the impossible map and checked it again. 'Hmm…'

The sketch drawn on it, though it was more from memory that his mind recreated the imagery, was slowly beginning to make sense.

There was the canyon pass that they'd just come through. Further up you could see the impossible mountain and the grasslands before them. It showed no trace of the stretch of woods before, or below, him. Maybe they were too insignificant?

The mountains were there as little more than a boundary to the less vertically challenged plains and hills and the darker greens of the forests. A lot of it was just empty space. The type where someone often scribbled, "Here Be Dragons" back in the day.[11]

So, what else was missing compared to what he could actually see in the landscape?

Glancing between the map and the reality before him, Seranthiem tried to familiarize himself with the area. He soon realized that he was missing a lot.

Most of all, the whole map didn't only lack evidence of the rest of the valley, it was hard to compare the sheer scale of the actual scenery. What he'd thought was just a bend around an outcrop looked, in reality, like it could have been the final outliner of a small mountain. He realized that all he could see when looking around him, no matter how he strained his eyes, was merely just a few squiggles on the map itself.

'Looks like we'll be doing a bit of camping out tonight, Wave,' Sam said stoically. 'I don't think we'll have any chance of reaching the stables we're looking for any time soon. Let's see if we can find somewhere to wash off all this dust while we're at it.'

He clucked at the horse, urging the stallion down a barely passable trail leading downwards. Ever downwards.

One thing was certain, Seranthiem thought. This was going to be a very different experience than he had imagined.

---

[11] These days, this would be the Dragon Research Centre. Very much *not* unknown and most definitely not hard to miss due to its size — dragons not being the smallest of beings.

Acknowledgements

High Fyelds' journey started many, many moons ago now, long before it was even called High Fyelds. In light of that, I'd like to thank HARPG for many years of fun and laughter and general shenanigans.

FlyingGekko once again chose to trust me with one of her characters via the "create your own character tier" at the time of the launch of "The Damsel and the Dragon" and I hope you all like him. Mordjen is a sweetie, even if you'd probably run very far, very fast, if you ever met him in a dark alley ;-)

Again, a huge thanks goes out to my cover artist, Juliane Völker, who valiantly took on the challenge of drawing horses, instead of the dragons we both love and adore, for both of the first "High Fyelds" books.

And an ever huger thanks (and extra huggles) for my brilliant editor, Ashley Lachance for putting up with me. I'm so sorry for all the horrible comma gremlins and their ilk that I subjected you to in this manuscript. I swear they multiply when I'm not looking.

Equal thanks go to my wonderful readers, Wanda Aasen, Lark Cunningham, Aramanth Dawe, Elizabeth-Rose Best, Skywings14, Tyler Richter, Ashli T, Tasha Turner, Scott Schaper, Rhonda Harms and Rhel ná DecVandé, who helped launch this out into the world. This wouldn't be nearly as fun without you all :)

I should probably thank the Muse too. The Little Darling has been bombarding me with ideas for future books even as I was trying to finish-up this one.

Chrono-order of the Seven of Stars novels

Seven of Stars isn't written chronologically (you can blame the Muse for that), so if you'd like to read the books in the order they actually take place within their universe, this won't be the order in which they were published. The good thing is, you don't *need* to read them in any particular order to enjoy them.

The universe itself is divided into seven different **Ages**.

1st Age -3rd Age

4th Age
"The Damsel and the Dragon"
"Magical Mischief"
"You're a Dragon" (coming in 2018)

5th Age
"The Dawn of the Winds"
"Wolf's Bane"

6th Age
"The Soul Within" (coming 2019)
"High Fyelds – A New Beginning"
"High Fyelds – The Big Race"

7th Age
"Academia Draconia"

The Damsel and the Dragon

Or so the sages say. Linandra isn't so sure.

Maybe that's because, unlike most sages', Lin's life actually contains dragons. Several of them.

But they don't cause anywhere near as much trouble as the wizards, mages, sorcerers and other arcane users that inhabits her new home.

Welcome to the Twin Towers.

Mae McKinnon

DragonQuill Publishing

Do YOU have what it takes to face your fears?

THEN JOIN THE DRAGONCORPS
AND PROTECT THE SKIES
OF NEW RETMIA!

Academia Draconia

The school where courage matters!

For Gaile Ashworthey and her fellow students, getting into the Dragon Research Centre had been easy.

. The hard part was staying long enough to graduate.

Trouble is, Gaile has a terrible head for heights. Not to mention, she's not big on teamwork.

But teamwork is what a dragon and rider is all about. If she's going to find a partner, it's going to take a dragon unlike any other.

Mae McKinnon

 DragonQuill Publishing

HIGH FIELDS

A NEW BEGINNING

When Erina has to trade her spaceship for a horse, it opens up a whole new world - literally.

Now she's lost in a place that shouldn't exist. The electronics refuse to work. And there is something lurking in the dark.

It's a good thing the horses seem friendly.

But in Darklight Valley nothing is what it appears to be.

Not the horses.
Not the monsters.
Not even Erina.

Mae McKinnon

DRAGONQUILL PUBLISHING

www.ingramcontent.com/pod-product-compliance
Lightning Source LLC
Chambersburg PA
CBHW020322130626
46549CB00003B/968